Helen Cresswell was born in Nottinghamshire and educated at Nottingham Girls' High School and King's College, London, where she took a degree in English. She has been writing from the age of seven, and is the author of many successful children's books including *The Piemakers* and *The Night-watchmen*, for which she won the Phoenix Award in 1988. Two of her most popular titles, *The Secret World of Polly Flint* and *Moondial*, were planned as television serials as well as books, and Helen Cresswell wrote the screenplays for both.

UP THE PIER

Helen Cresswell

Illustrated by Gareth Floyd

faber and faber

LONDON · BOSTON

First published in Great Britain in 1971
by Faber and Faber Limited
3 Queen Square London WC1N 3AU
This paperback edition first published in 1989

Printed in Great Britain by
Richard Clay Ltd, Bungay, Suffolk

*A CIP record for this book is available from the
British Library*

ISBN 0-571-14187-0

For Phyllis Hunt

Prologue

On 1 October 1971 the six-forty-seven train from London drew into Llangolly station at six-forty-nine precisely. Nobody seemed to take very much notice. The season was over. There was not a sign of a porter and no hollowed voice over the loudspeaker to announce its coming. The rain beat down, puckering the puddles on Platform One and blurring the lighted carriage windows so that you could not even see the reassuring faces of passengers pressed against them.

A middle-aged woman stood in the shelter of the waiting-room door, looking up and down the platform. A carriage door swung open and she stepped forward eagerly. Two men, a woman and a boy alighted. The watcher stepped back again, disappointed.

Then, from the other direction, the figures she was searching for evidently appeared. She put up her umbrella and hurried forward to meet the woman and small girl who stood looking about them, pale and saucer-eyed under the old-fashioned iron street lamp that lit the further end of the platform. They seemed not to notice the rain at all. A minute later the figures merged as they embraced, and then they all set off back together, their faces concealed behind the umbrella tilted against the driving rain.

At the ticket office they waited while the other little group of passengers showed their tickets and went through the barrier.

If you had been a seagull that night, riding high on the windy gusts above the lights of the little town, you might have watched the passengers going their separate ways.

You would have seen the two women and the girl climb into a waiting car. You would have followed its winding progress through the empty streets, its headlights cutting across the rain, slicing it out of the dark. Until at last it stopped outside a tall house with stone steps leading up to the front door.

Being a seagull, you would not have been able to read the words above the door and the arch of unlit fairy lights, CRAIG LEA PRIVATE HOTEL, and once the three figures had mounted the steps and the door closed behind them, you would have lost interest, and naturally so.

But if you were a particularly curious seagull, you could then have winged your way back towards the station and rediscovered the other four, making their way on foot towards the sea front. They had no umbrella, and their heads were bent against the rain that came blowing in from the sea. When they reached the sea front, instead of following the curved promenade and its rows of hotels with darkened windows, they crossed the road and made for a tiny light that burned in a small stone house that stood at the entrance to the pier itself.

Hovering overhead you would have seen them knock, the door open and a band of light flooding their faces and for a moment, above the roar of the wind and sea, you would have heard the astonished cry of the man who had opened to them. Then the door closed, and they were gone.

After this, most gulls would have called it a day, and sought their eyrie among the crags of the Great Strindel that loomed behind the pier and soared into the darkness above the little town. But let us say that you were the kind of seagull whose curiosity knew no bounds, and that you perched on a nearby railing, and waited.

You would have waited a long time—two hours, perhaps, or even three—and would be nodding on your perch when at last the door opened again and this time five figures emerged, closing the door behind them. One of them stooped to unlock a gate, and they all passed through and began to walk down the pier away from the light and into the blackness beyond.

Being a seagull, you would pride yourself on the unusual sharpness of your eyes, and when those five figures seemed suddenly to—vanish?—from one moment to the next, you would hardly think it possible. You would have dived and soared over the spot where they disappeared, shrieking and cawking your displeasure, and rousing answering cries from the slumbering gulls among the rocks.

At last you would fly off, sullen and cheated. Which is a pity. Because if you had waited, you would have seen those five figures reappear as suddenly as they had vanished, and walk rapidly back to the pier entrance. And this would have made you feel very much better. A pity, but there you are. Patience was never a seagull's strong suit.

In any case, perhaps you knew that it would all happen again, and that you could afford to wait until tomorrow. . . .

Chapter One

Carrie was woken by the screaming of gulls. She lay there for several minutes before she realized what the din was, and then she did remember, and knew, all in a rush, where she was. Even then she did not move, but lay half-stunned by the noise that seemed to be a continuation of the thrumming of the train the day before, whose rhythm still ran in her head.

She lay moving only her eyes, exploring the strange room.

"Not one of my best," Aunt Ester had explained the night before. "But I thought a small one'd suit her better. No point opening up the big rooms, this time of year. Get the gas fire going in here and it'll be cosy in no time."

She'd been lighting up the fire as she spoke, and Carrie had been grateful for its instant warmth and glow. She'd actually fallen asleep by its reddish light, so someone must have come in later and turned it off.

Her eyes continued to roam the room, taking in the huge wardrobe and dressing-table, the little bedside lamp, the printed notice hung on the back of the door, the luggage rack with her own cases and boxes un-opened on top.

"All the things I've got in the world," she thought, and was terrified, because they seemed so little.

There was no home now, nowhere to go, and all the treasures and possessions of her ten years lay in those few boxes. She wanted to jump up and run to them and unpack them, all of them, to recognize familiar faces and books, to reach for their reassurance in this strange, bare room.

But perhaps it wasn't even worth unpacking, because even this was not to be home, but only a stopping place, a kind of waiting-room between home and home.

Carrie closed her eyes and conjured up her own house, her real home, and tried to imagine it still there in the busy street with the milk bottles clattering and the children shouting on the way to school. She managed the trick, she could see it quite clearly in every detail, but even this did not help. She couldn't quite manage to blot out the sign that said For Sale and had stood in the front garden for months after her father had gone away to his new job. Then, for a short while, the sign had said Sold, and from then onwards she had felt her old world slipping away from her.

Even her friends had suddenly become strangers and over-polite because once the house was sold she did not really belong there any more, was there on false pre-tences.

Now there was to be a pause between homes, a whole fortnight with this cousin of her mother's.

"We'll start somewhere new," her mother had said. "Just the three of us."

It had sounded frightening and at the same time exciting. "Just the three of us . . ." as if the whole world were a wilderness and the three of them pioneers. Or only the *two* of them, really, because over the months her father had become only a voice over a crackling, long-distance line. Even the voice she hardly recognized, asking questions and saying the kind of things that her father would never have said if he were actually there with her, face to face.

Now, lying in this high, yellow-painted room and lazily tracing the cracks on the wash-basin with her eyes, Carrie felt not at all a pioneer. Surely *this* could not be the start of the great adventure? For a time, yesterday, on the train, racing between the ploughed autumn fields and coppery woods, it had *seemed* like the start of something wonderful and strange. She remembered that towards the end, after nearly five hours of travelling, she had longed for the train not to arrive at all. She had wanted to go on and on forever, flying through the unfamiliar, darkening landscape, poised forever in time and space, and had dreaded the anticlimax of arrival.

She hardly remembered the arrival now at all, it had the vagueness and unreality of a dream. She remembered the rain and the drive from the station, the greetings in the warm basement kitchen, the hot drink, the climb up the strangely steep stairs to her room. It was all blurred and commonplace and everyday, not at all what the start of a new life should be.

Still, there were the gulls. She listened again to them now with wide-awake ears and slowly, with a rising excitement, remembered that she was by the sea. She stared at the glow behind the flowered chintz that meant the sun was up. Suddenly she had to know what lay behind and with a swift leap was out of bed and hopping over the cold lino and pulling the curtains wide apart and blinking in the strong light.

She had really no idea what she had expected to see, and what she did see forced a little cry of surprise and pleasure from her lips. The hotel was perched on the mountainside and she was looking down over wet, shining grey-tiled roofs, blindingly reflecting the early sun. The foreground was all roofs and walls of stone and pebble and beyond were the sea and sky over the wide estuary, a bright band of wateriness and reflections. Birds wheeled and swung over the shining flats. Behind the little town the hills were auburn and gold with bracken and turning fern, broken here and there by grey, weather-bitten boulders.

"The Strindel Stones," Carrie thought. Her mother had told her about them. Centuries ago they had been rolled by a giant down the very mountain that rose behind Craig Lea—the Great Strindel.

At the near side of the bay she could see the pier with its white-painted kiosks striding out over the greenish waves, and because the tide was out, standing half on land, half on sea, like some strange amphibious creature. As she watched, by some trick of the light, a small figure seemed suddenly to appear out of nowhere, walking up the pier towards land. It was a boy, and he paused for a moment to put down something he was carrying in his arms. A dog bounded off and ran sniffing about him, and next minute both boy and dog were hidden from view behind the roofs and chimneys.

"It'll be all right," Carrie found herself thinking. "Everything'll be all right."

When she came down for breakfast Aunt Ester was lecturing on the hardships and pitfalls of running a seaside hotel. Carrie herself sat silent, and as soon as she had finished went back up to her room. She read the list of commands hanging on the door of her room, and could practically hear Aunt Ester reading them aloud with her over her shoulder. It was all about things like not moving furniture and scratching the lino and not leaving lights on on the landing and cleaning the bath when you'd used it. Carrie turned the list over to the blank side, and felt better.

An hour later she was running down the stone steps, then stopping to look about her at the bright Welsh morning. And that was another thing.

"I'm in a foreign country," she thought. "Wales. Will they speak Welsh, I wonder?"

She looked back up at the house and saw the Great Strindel rearing behind it, almost vertically like a great sloping wall. From the back rooms of the hotel she had already found that the only view was of the side of the mountain, and had had to crouch down low to see the sky at all. Peering into a room on the top floor she had come face to face with a shaggy mountain goat level with the window, and they had stared at one another, startled by the encounter.

Carrie followed the downward slope of the road that would take her to the sea. It was a narrow, curving street with high kerbs and steep pavements lined with little shops that spilled out into the street, and tall stone houses, shoulder to shoulder. From a corner of her eye, as she began to run, she saw railings flash by and guessed that this was the school yard, barred like a prison. Then the bay appeared suddenly from behind a corner, taking her by surprise.

The pier entrance was almost opposite and she crossed over, feeling all at once the strangeness of being in a seaside town that was deserted. She could have gone down the seaweed-strewn steps to the sea and paddled her way right to the far end of the bay, and for a minute she was tempted. But somehow

there did not seem much point to it when no one else was about.

A sign at the pier gate said "Adults 5p—Children 2½p" and Carrie paused and fished in her pocket. There was no one in the little ticket office. Carrie looked about her, then pressed against the turnstile. It did not move.

"Just a minute. Just a *minute*."

A testy voice from the right made her jump. A very small, very old man was standing there. He was collarless, tieless, and wore a peaked black cap that said "Llangolly Pier" in gold lettering.

"You're up early," he remarked, noisily unlocking the office door. "Don't reckon on folk this early, out of season."

"Sorry," Carrie said.

"O, you're within your *rights*," he said, inside the little hut now and unlocking a drawer. "Pier's *open*, all right. It's just that I don't *reckon* on customers this early, October, and why should I? So I take to having breakfast late, d'ye see, and you've caught me with my sleeves rolled up."

"I'm not your first customer, anyway, am I?" said Carrie, suddenly remembering the boy she had seen earlier.

"Eh? Not the first? That you are, missy, by a long chalk."

"What about that boy?" said Carrie.

"Boy?" He looked blank.

"Yes, that boy with a dog. I saw them from my window ages ago—before breakfast."

"Dog," repeated the old man. "*Dog*? There's no dogs allowed on this pier, Missy, and Samuel Pontifex isn't the man to go breaking Company rules."

"But I *saw* them," persisted Carrie. "A boy and a dog. Walking towards this end. Really I did."

He shook his head and held out a hand for the money.

She put it on the counter and he gave her a ticket from a huge roll.

"Must've been the sun," he said. "Plays queer tricks, the sun does. Sun on water'll make something out of nothing real as life. Off you go now."

The turnstile clicked and Carrie went through. She was still on tarmac, the pier proper did not begin for a long way yet, and on her left reared the crags of the Strindel. It was not quiet enough for Carrie to feel lonely. The gulls dipped and rose and figured the salt air and the sea dashed into white spray on the wet black rocks.

Suddenly she was excited by it all and began to run. She ran towards the line that divided the land pier from the sea pier, the tarmac from the wooden deck. And as she took a last long stride over the dividing line, she saw the dog.

Chapter Two

It was running round in circles and barking furiously a few yards ahead. And as if its excitement were infectious the gulls, too, were thrown into panic and hovered uneasily with hoarse, protesting cries.

Carrie held out a hand.

"Come on, boy," she said softly. "Good boy. Come on."

The dog stiffened and turned, and if a dog can stare, then it *stared*, its eyes dilated and ears laid back.

"Come on," said Carrie again, doubtfully this time—wasn't it a bad sign when dogs put back their ears? But her presence seemed to have filled the animal with renewed frenzy, and he had thrown himself into his whirligig pattern again, covering the same few inches over and over in a kind of mad dance, as if he were prancing round someone's feet. Except, of course, that there was no one there.

"Hey, boy!" cried Carrie. "Here!"

But she might as well not have existed. She stood there, and the dog whirled and the gulls whirled and all the sudden noise and movement and panic were a mystery, quite inexplicable. Carrie had the extra-ordinary feeling that she was shut out of something, that the dog and the gulls were in league, were sharing the same secret.

Suddenly angry, she walked away.

"Stupid," she muttered. "Stupid dog."

Between the boards under her feet she suddenly caught sight of the sea, boiling between the iron legs of

the pier. She walked mesmerized by it for a way, and by the time she lifted her eyes again she had almost forgotten the dog. She was level with the first pair of kiosks, one on either hand.

The windows of the one on her right were full of photographs, and she went over and looked curiously at them. They were all snaps of people walking on the pier, mothers, fathers, lovers, children, all caught in space and time by the click of a shutter, and all gone now, leaving only their images behind. Carrie stared into the sheepishly-smiling, anonymous faces, and wondered where they all were now, and whether they knew that part of them had stayed behind, to winter on Llangolly pier.

Then a batch of photographs on the door itself caught her eye. A handwritten sign above them said "A. Hanbury, Photographs. Established Fifty Years." Coming up the pier were men with whiskers and brimmed hats, men wearing striped blazers and white shoes. With them were ladies with long, tube-like dresses, loops of beads and pudding-basin hats. The boys wore sailor suits and the girls were prim and unsmiling little replicas of their mothers. Carrie stared at them. They were no more real —or unreal—than the trippers of 1971, all alike were poised forever in time, trapped by the camera.

She turned away and looked at the kiosk opposite. Newspapers covered all the windows, giving it a blank, anonymous look. On the door hung a notice "TO LET".

Carrie walked on. She watched the sea curdling away down below till the monotonous sliding away of the narrow planks under her gaze made her feel giddy and rather sick. She looked up again and saw that she had reached the second pair of kiosks. The one on the left was shuttered, and the sign above the door read "Madame Lucille, Palmist". The other, its windows crowded with Welsh dolls, shiny brass and postcards, belonged to J. Jones, Souvenirs.

She ran on to the last pair of kiosks, feeling the boards spring a little under her weight—surely they only *seemed* to bounce? The kiosk on the left was brown-papered and "To Let". The other was crammed with black and white silhouette portraits and belonged to

J. Jones. She went right round the kiosk on the narrow balcony and found that J. Jones dabbled in water colours, too. The back window was filled with paintings of Llangolly and the Great Strindel. Some of them were dated as far back as the 1930s and 1940s, and it was clear that the trade in wishy-washy watercolours was far from brisk.

Carrie looked back down the pier and far away she could see the dog still weaving his strange, urgent dance, and the seagulls hovering over the spot. Again she washed her hands of them and walked on to the shabby white Pier Pavilion. From the distance it had looked magical, magnificent, like an oriental palace or Magician's folly. Now she saw it as peeled and blistering, ringed by litter bins and faded posters. She knelt on the wooden bench that ran round it and stared through the glass at the empty rows of red plush seats and the array of music stands on the stage.

There was nothing left to do now but walk right to the very end of the pier, behind the pavilion itself, out of sight of land. Carrie leaned over the rail and counted ships on the horizon. Then she stared down at the sea for a few minutes, and then there was nothing left to do at all. She turned and began to retrace her steps.

She was half-way between land and sea, nearly level with the first pair of kiosks, when she suddenly realized that the dog had gone. She might not have remembered it at all had it not been for the gulls. A dozen or so of them were still diving and shrieking, diving and shrieking, over and over again above her head.

Carrie stopped for a minute, mystified, looking about

her. What could it be? On her left was the photograph kiosk, on her right the one that was empty TO LET, its doors and windows covered with newspaper. She went over to it and walked right round it, peering to see if she could find a crack in the paper blinds.

As she did so, she caught sight of a photograph that seemed familiar. It was of a fox cub that had been reared by hand by a Devon farmer. Her mother had shown it to her only a few days before. Carrie tilted her head sideways and read the date at the top of the newspaper. 29 September. So the windows of the kiosk had been papered only in the last day or two? She wondered idly why they had been papered at all. An empty kiosk is an empty kiosk, and that was all there was to it. She went all round it once more in a last hope of finding a chink.

Disappointed, she carried on walking back to the empty shore. At the turnstile there was no sign of the gatekeeper, so she couldn't even ask *him* about the dog. She walked away along the promenade with a curious sense of flatness, as if she really had been at sea, and had to find her land legs again. Llangolly was strange and unfamiliar and she felt like a foreigner in the steep cobbled sideways-leaning alleys of crabbed cottages with lace-net-covered windows and high stone steps. The washing flapped behind them and women gabbled over the walls in high Welsh voices. But no children played on the hop-scotch-marked pavements, and to Carrie the morning seemed empty and unpeopled for all the busy comings and goings. In the end she wandered reluctantly back to Craig Lea and sat waiting for her dinner in the basement kitchen.

That afternoon her mother and Aunt Ester had visitors in to play whist while Carrie went down to the beach. She was not allowed to bathe while she was by herself, so she meant to paddle the whole length of the bay—a mile or more. Here and there elderly ladies sauntered in pairs, but the beach itself was deserted.

Or so Carrie thought. The first thing she saw as she jumped the few feet from the concrete down to the beach was the dog. He was just running from under the pier itself, his coat wet and bedraggled, barking excitedly. Just behind him, leaping gingerly over the shingle, was a boy.

"Hey!" cried Carrie. The boy stopped and turned. She clapped a hand to her mouth. Why on earth had she called like that? What should she say?

"I'm—I'm sorry," she said. "I thought you were somebody else."

"Who?" asked the boy disconcertingly.

"I—I don't know. Just somebody."

He continued to stand there, staring at her, and she plucked up courage to go on.

"It was really your dog I recognized," she said.

"Muff?"

"Is that his name?"

" 'Course. Muff, here boy! Good boy! Here!"

The dog turned and bounded back towards them, tongue lolling. He began to dance excitedly about the boy's feet. Carrie recognized the dance.

"I saw him this morning," she said. "On the pier. I thought he was lost."

"On the pier?" the boy said. "On the pier? Dogs isn't allowed on the pier."

His face was alert and watchful now, and Carrie suddenly knew quite certainly that if she insisted, if she went on talking about the dog and the pier, the boy would go, probably for good.

"Well, I thought I saw him," she said. "But I must've been wrong."

"Must've."

They stood looking at one another. The boy was sandy-haired with freckles, and golden eyelashes over bright blue eyes. He was wearing a jersey much too big for him and clumsy tweed trousers rolled up to his knees.

"Why aren't you at school?" Carrie asked, and could have bitten off her tongue because the boy's face was guarded again, suspicious, almost.

"Why ain't you?" he countered.

"Because I don't belong here. At least, not for certain. I might be stopping and I might not, we don't know for sure. And anyway, I haven't had a proper holiday so my mother said I could have two weeks off."

The boy bent and picked up a flat stone and sent it skimming expertly over the waves. It waltzed over the surface and leapt several times before it sank. Carrie advanced and stood watching while he repeated the trick several times.

"You're good at it," she said at last.

He shrugged.

"Nothing to it."

"*I* can't do it."

"You're a girl." He didn't sound exactly scornful, more pitying. Carrie sat down and pulled off her sandals.

"I'm going to paddle right along to the far side," she told him. It was the nearest she dared go towards an invitation.

"Are you? Come on, Muff. Here, boy!"

"Are you going home?" she asked.

"Sort of. Come on, boy! Heel!"

He swung round with a swift salute.

"Bye!" he called, and was off again, back the way he had come, under the pier.

Carrie picked up her sandals and minced over the gravel to the sea's edge. Once or twice she turned and looked back over her shoulder, but of the boy and his dog there was not a sign. She realized that she knew not

a single thing about them, except the dog's name—
Muff.

When she had paddled for more than half a mile she
turned and looked back again. The beach was deserted.
But something else caught her eye. Above the pier,
level with the first pair of kiosks, was a swarm of gulls.
Even from that distance she could hear their faint shrieks
blown sideways on the wind, and see their frantic
plunging and soaring.

The gulls of Llangolly were in a fine stew about something. About what, Carrie did not know, but she had a fortnight in which to find out.

"And the first thing to do," she decided, paddling on, "is to buy a season ticket for the pier."

As it turned out, what she bought was more than just a season ticket. It was a passport, too.

Chapter Three

Mr Pontifex looked surprised when Carrie came down to the pier again that day. Straight after tea she raced down towards the sea, knowing that there was only an hour or two of daylight left. Already she was familiar with the way, had made a small corner of Llangolly her own.

The gatekeeper was even more surprised when Carrie asked for a season ticket.

"Season?" he echoed. "The season's over, missy."

"I mean the *winter* season," she said firmly. She had half expected this. She felt certain that there was some mysterious link between him and the dog and boy. Why else should he have pretended not to have seen them?

"Staying long, then?" he asked, rummaging in his drawer.

"I don't know," she replied truthfully. "I may be, and I may not."

"Shouldn't have thought there was much on a pier for a young 'un, this time of year," he went on. "If it's slot machines you're after, there's an arcade in the Queen's Road."

"Oh, it's not the slot machines," Carrie said. "I didn't even notice there were any. You know that kiosk on the left, the first one along?"

He looked up.

"Has it been empty long?"

"All summer," he said. "Piers ain't what they were, these days. There's not the same call for them."

Carrie was hardly listening. She was thinking, "Empty all summer, yet the newspapers were put over the windows in the last day or two. Why?"

"Ah, when I was a lad, that was the days for piers," went on the old man. "Fifty year ago and more, a pier was a pier then. Like a world of its own, it was. I come of a pier family, you know. The day was when Llangolly pier was Pontifex from top to bottom, as you might say."

He sighed.

"There's a mad fool I was, when I was young. Ran off to sea when I was but fifteen. Gone twenty year and more I was, all told. And when I come back—"

He spread his fingers and shrugged.

"What?"

"Gone. All of 'em. As I might have knowed they'd be, I s'pose. Always on the move, pier folk."

"Oh! How terrible!" Carrie cried. "And did you never find them?"

"Never, missy. Didn't try. I'd run off from 'em, see, and hardly liked to face 'em. Only lately I've thought of 'em much at all. Must be getting old—dreaming about the old days. Fifty year and not so much as a whisper of 'em, then—"

He broke off suddenly.

"Here we are. Don't lose it." He pushed the ticket towards her over the counter. "Not going down to-night, are you?"

She nodded.

"Lights don't go on," he warned. "Not after September 30th. Don't you get left down there in the dark."

"I won't," she said.

She began to walk rapidly away, eager to reach the wooden deck, the *real* pier. A slow autumn dusk was already gathering and the line between sea and sky was blurred on the horizon. The gulls were quiet now, the clamour of the morning forgotten. She noticed that only an odd one here and there smoothly rode the quiet evening air, *swam* in it, as if it were deep water.

Carrie's pace slackened. All at once she felt that she had been mistaken, that there *was* no mystery, that the pier was as empty as it seemed to be, shuttered against the coming of the winter. None the less, something seemed to draw her on, and looking down she saw that she had already reached the line where wood and tarmac met.

Playing an old, childish game, she kept her eyes fixed downwards and began to tread the boards in a ritual pattern. She carefully stepped with the ball of her foot each time on every third plank, tiptoeing to keep her foot clear of the others as if her life depended on it. But the planks were narrow and her balance unsteady, and after the first few steps she felt herself swaying and threw out her arms to balance herself. In vain. Her

foot missed the allotted plank and the rhythm was broken.

She lifted her head and saw for the first time that she was not alone. A little group of figures stood by the first kiosk, the empty one, and a dog sat watching close by.

She stared at them and they stared back, and as their gazes met and locked, part of her mind was suddenly aware that one of the figures was the boy she had met on the beach, and another part was that the seagulls had been thrown into panic again. All in a moment they had come crowding from their hideouts in the Strindel and set up a coarse, deafening clamour right above Carrie's head, throwing her into a kind of daze.

Then she saw that the watching faces had changed now, they wore expressions of bewilderment, even alarm, and the man and the woman exchanged uneasy glances.

"George," said the young woman in a low voice, "she ain't *seeing* us, surely?"

"Seems to." The man gave Carrie another hard look. "Straight at us, she's looking. I could swear she's seeing us."

"What's gone wrong?" wailed the woman then. "What'll we do?"

"Hold steady, Ellen," the man said. "Wait. See what happens."

Carrie shifted her gaze back to the boy. He too stood watching, wordless and alert. She suddenly knew that they might stand there for ever, all four of them, locked in an endless stare, unless she herself made the first move. They were waiting for *her*.

"Hello," she heard her own voice croak, and it sounded so hoarse and far away, so lost amid the shrieking of the gulls, that she cleared her throat and said it again, "Hello!", so loudly this time that it came out as a shout.

"She *do* see us!" cried the woman then, and clutched at the man's sleeve. "Oh—whatever? What'll we do?"

"It's the same one, pa," the boy said then. "The one who was down this morning, remember? The one on the beach I told you about. She's on to us, pa! Must be!"

Looking into those three faces, frightened and aghast, became almost unbearable. They were looking at her as if she were some kind of monster. Pleadingly she stretched out a hand.

"What's wrong?" she cried. "What have I done?"

They did not answer. If anything, she seemed to have made matters worse.

"She sees us *and* hears us," said the man, and his voice was not quite steady. "But it's not the end of things. Just keep calm, and act natural."

He, too, cleared his throat.

"Evening," he said, and this time he was speaking direct to Carrie.

"Good evening!" she cried, weak with relief, feeling human again.

"There you are," said the man to the woman. "Answers straight back, you see."

"Why does he keep talking as if I'm not here?" wondered Carrie desperately. "What's *happening*?"

"If we act natural, we might win through yet," the man went on. "You say something to her"—nudging the boy.

"Had a good paddle this afternoon, did you?" asked the boy obediently.

"O yes, thank you!" Carrie cried.

"Me and Muff went rock climbing," he went on.

"We was just having a last stroll down the pier," the man put in quickly, frowning at the boy as if to warn him not to say too much.

"N-nice evening for a stroll," the woman managed.

"Lovely," agreed Carrie warmly. She heard the tremor in the voice, and willed the woman not to be afraid of her.

"It's lovely," she said again.

Just then the dog rose, stretched, and padded towards Carrie. He sniffed and wagged his tail and Carrie, grateful for at least this show of friendship, bent and patted his head.

"Good dog, Muff," she said, and now her voice trembled, too.

"We'll be getting along, then," said the man. He took the woman's arm firmly and motioned to the boy with his head. "'Night, missy."

"Oh—goodbye!" Carrie cried. Were they really going? And where? All she could do herself now was begin to walk away from them, up the pier. After a few yards she turned and looked back. They were all still standing there in a close-knit group, watching. Hastily the man threw up a hand in a half-wave, pulled at the woman's arm and began walking determinedly in the opposite direction. The boy gave her a final, curious stare, and followed suit.

After that, Carrie dared not look back again. Already they saw her as someone dangerous, perhaps as a spy.

"But why?" she thought, and found herself saying the words out loud. "Why?"

Then, too, there was the strange witness of the gulls. *They* knew that something mysterious was afoot on Llangolly pier. She could still hear their clamour following after.

Right to the very end of the pier she walked, into the gathering dusk, and stood watching the tiny lights of ships far out on the sea's rim. There she went over the encounter in her mind, looking for clues.

Oddly enough, now that she could no longer actually *see* the trio, she was more aware of their appearance. There had been something strange about them, even apart from their hard gaze and pale, frightened faces. Something . . . something that she could hardly place— was it to do with the clothes they were wearing? Try as she might, she could not remember their costume except as a vague impression—it was the faces she could still see in her mind's eye, and the watchful eyes. But the longer she thought, the more she felt certain that there *had* been something odd about their dress, something vaguely old-fashioned and out of date.

Now the light had nearly gone and Carrie remembered that she had promised to be back at Craig Lea before dark. She set back towards land at a run. As she ran she could see a few lights here and there along the margin of the bay, but the pier itself, as Mr Pontifex had warned her, was in darkness. The festoons of fairylights hung dead and dark as stones between the lamp-posts.

She did not pause for breath until she reached the first pair of kiosks, and then she halted for a moment, hearing her own breathing and the regular rise and fall of the waves below. The gulls had evidently screeched themselves into silence and taken off to their perches in the Strindel. The little kiosks stood blank and shuttered.

Of the strange trio there was not a sign. They had vanished. Of that, Carrie felt certain. Wherever they had gone, they had simply vanished.

She went on walking. As she left the deck behind and set foot on land again, a single, solitary gull perched on the railings let out a shrill, startled cry and flew up, circling overhead and rousing answering cries from the nearby rocks.

Scared by the harsh cry out of the dark Carrie began to run again. The gull followed, scolding noisily. Only as she pushed through the turnstile and stood panting on the promenade did it make a final, wheeling dive and fly off, merging into the gloom.

Carrie stared after it, and as she stood there, suddenly felt that she was being watched. She turned towards the little stone gatehouse and for a fraction of a second was certain that she saw the curtains at the lighted window stir and settle, as if somebody had been peering between them....

She began to run again, this time not stopping till she reached the bottom of the stone steps outside the hotel. Craig Lea might not be home, but at least it was safety....

Chapter Four

The smell that rose from under the pier was strong and cold, a wet-stone, wet-weed, wet-sand smell. It was a smell of age and yet fresh and salty, and to Carrie it was beginning to be the smell of excitement. By ten o'clock, just as the morning mist was dissolving and the heavy dew drying, she was back on the still damp boards, eyes fixed on that first white kiosk and its blank, newspapered windows.

She sniffed in the cold air gladly, ridding her nostrils of the smell of dust and wax polish and who-knows-what-scented air-fresheners that hung in the high, silent rooms of Craig Lea. She had earned her freedom that day, had dusted the empty bedrooms, mopped their cold brown lino and run to the grocers and back twice for Aunt Pester. (She had decided that this was how she would think of her aunt in her own mind. It put her at a satisfying distance—in her place, in fact.)

So virtuous did she feel, so deserving of reward, that it was with a curious sense of flatness that she stood now staring at the spot where she had expected to find *something*—what, she did not know. Even the gulls were in workaday mood—diving, flying, sitting on rails, their world intact and unalarmed. It was a plain, peaceful October morning with everything in its right place, and Carrie felt betrayed.

She crossed to the other kiosk, the one with the photographs, and gazed at the old summer scenes. The pictures on the door caught her eye again, and something about them made her look more closely. "Llangolly Pier Fifty Years Ago" a caption read. But it was a strange familiarity about the pictures themselves that held her, though at first it eluded her, maddeningly, like a half-forgotten tune. She stared at the brownish prints of thin ladies in tube dresses, moustached men and poker-faced children, straining to capture the mislaid likeness. And when it came it was in a flash, and she let out a cry of recognition.

It was the clothes! That was it—that was what she had half known the night before—that strange, frightened trio she had met only a few yards from where she was standing now—these were the clothes they had been wearing! She was certain of it—she could see again the silhouette of the woman, long and narrow, and of the man's trousers, caught in below the knee like plus-fours. He had even worn a moustache!

At that very moment, as if in sympathy, the gulls went into storm again, but by now Carrie was past noticing. Her eye had fallen on one particular print, right on the bottom row, in the middle. Three figures stared solemnly back at her as they had stared into the camera lens half a century ago. A man, a woman and a boy. *Them.*

Carrie let out a long, gasping breath.

"Hello," said a voice behind her.

She whirled round. It was the boy. He wore a ring of angry gulls like a halo. She stared into his unmistakably live face, speechless. He had stepped out of that sepia print, flesh and blood, and was now regarding her with a long, curious stare for all the world as if it were *she* who was the ghost.

"Hello," he said again.

Still she could not bring herself to answer. One simply could not say "Hello" to a ghost.

"Look as if you've seen a ghost," he said.

She clapped a hand to her mouth.

"What's up? Lost your tongue?"

She shook her head. But she had.

"Look, if you don't want to talk, don't. Thought you did, yesterday. Thought you—oh, never mind!"

He turned as if to go and she put out a swift hand and cried "No, stop!" and he turned back expectantly.

"Don't go! You gave me a fright, that's all, coming up behind me like that. And the—" she looked round wildly—"and the gulls making all that noise, and everything!"

"O *them!* I wish they'd shut it. You can't hardly put your nose out the door without them setting up."

"Which door?" Carrie almost asked—but didn't.

He cupped his hands round his mouth and yelled "Clear off! Go on, d'ye hear me—clear off!"

Carrie let out a high, nervous giggle. He scowled.

"It's not your life they're plaguing out of you," he said.

42

"They were yesterday. Yesterday they did it to me as well."

"Ah!" He gave her a hard look. "Yesterday."

She hardly knew what she was expected to say, so she waited.

"That was when you come down here the second time," he went on.

"But how do you know?" she cried. "You weren't there in the morning. It was your dog that was there then, and it was him who'd set the gulls off." She glanced swiftly about. "Where's he now? Where's Muff?"

He shrugged.

"Somewhere about. Not far off."

"*I* can't see him."

"Ah, but then you *don't* see everything, do you?" he said.

"I see most things, usually," she said stiffly. This boy seemed always to turn the tables on her. "I notice quite a lot of things."

He said nothing.

"Like this photograph," she went on, feeling the hard thud of her heart. It had moved up into her mouth.

"Which?"

She pointed. He came up beside her and followed the direction of her finger. Then he let out a whistle.

"Jingo!" he cried. "It's us! Well, beat that! It's ma and pa and me!"

He seemed delighted. She had played what she thought was her trump card, and he had turned not a single carrotty hair.

"Don't you *know* what's happened?" she cried then,

because now *all* her cards might as well go down. "That picture was taken fifty years ago—look, it says so! And look at your clothes! You just stand there laughing, and you don't even belong here. *I* belong here, and you don't. You're from fifty years ago! You're—"

She broke off as he turned and gripped her arm hard.

"Ssssh!" he hissed. "Sssh! Not so loud!"

"But there's no one here!" she cried, looking about.

"Not that you can see. But ma's in there, asleep. If you carry on yowling you'll wake her, and then I'm for it!"

She looked at the little kiosk opposite. So she had been right. The newspaper blinds had a secret to hide. The kiosks had tenants for the winter—visible, invisible, who knew which?

"For all *I* know, she's up already," he went on, "and listening to every word I say." He faced the kiosk. "If you're listening, ma, don't you worry. Me and pa'll sort things out. You go back to sleep."

"I don't understand!" Carrie cried. "If she *is* there, why can't you see her?"

"Simple," he said. "I just undid the Three Times Seven."

"Just undid the what? Three Times Seven?"

"S'right. Hey, look, and so did Muff. Good boy, come on here."

His voice was almost lost in the renewed fury of the gulls. Carrie saw that the dog had appeared a few yards away from where they stood. He danced furiously about the boy's feet, then came to Carrie.

"He likes you. That's why I'm letting you in on things, partly. What's your name?"

"Carrie. Short for Caroline."

"Mine's Kitchener. Kitch, if you like."

They gave one another long, sizing looks. Now names had been exchanged and it was a serious business.

"Want to see something?"

She nodded.

"Come on, then. Come on, Muff."

He began to walk back towards land, and when he reached the line where the boards ended, stopped, and lifted the dog into his arms. Then he turned and faced back again the way he had come.

"Now for the Three Times Seven. S'easy, really. You must've done it yesterday without even knowing. Main thing is to keep tiptoe, so's your foot don't go on the wrong boards."

All at once she saw what he was talking about. She remembered her lurching, unsteady walk the day before, when she'd painstakingly trodden every third plank—seven times?

"Seven times?" she asked.

"S'right."

The whole thing was suddenly clear.

"And then we're invisible? *I* was invisible yesterday?"

"S'right."

"And that's why Muff—that's why you're holding him! He can't do it! And that's why I saw him yesterday!"

"S'right! Little tyke! He ran off the end here, see.

And that undoes it. Minute you get off the boards it's undone, see?"

"And that's why the gulls—"

"Look," he interrupted. "Are you coming or not?"

"Yes, I am, but—" she hesitated. "But—will *I* be back in 1921?"

"Look, I told you. You'll be invisible, that's all. It don't *hurt*, you know. Back in 1921? I wish it was that easy!"

Still she hung back. She looked about her at the still, sunlit morning, at the real water and the real town in the distance and lastly down at her own undeniably real feet. Could she take those ritual steps and still be real and in a real world? Could she be invisible and still *there*?

"I did it yesterday," she remembered. "Without even noticing the difference."

And Kitchener himself seemed to come and go as effortlessly as a shadow under a fickle sun. She looked at his face and caught a faint look of scorn and made up her mind.

"Ready," she said, and balanced her left foot carefully on the third plank. "One . . . two . . . three . . ."

After the seventh wavering step she lowered both feet on to the boards and looked at Kitchener who had finished before her. The gulls racketed overhead, the sun was still shining. She licked her dry lips with her tongue and found her tongue still wet and a flood of excitement and release rushed up.

"It's easy!" she cried.

But Kitchener was looking at something over her shoulder and turning she saw that a corner of one of the newspaper blinds had been lifted and a face was peering out at them. It was a white, wistful, tearstained face. It was Kitchener's mother.

"Other people's mothers cry, too," Carrie thought, and then the paper dropped over the window.

Chapter Five

"We've done it now," said Kitchener cheerfully. "Don't take any notice of her. She's jumpy, that's all."

"Jumpy?"

"Wouldn't you be? Fifty years on, and no way of getting back?"

"But you got *here*," said Carrie.

"Accidental," he retorted briefly. "We got here accidental."

"But how?" asked Carrie, wondering whatever kind of "accident" could pick you up and put you down fifty years hence without so much as a by-your-leave. The mere thought of it made life seem instantly more tricky, more dangerous than it had ever seemed before.

Before Kitchener could reply, the door of the kiosk opened. There stood the woman of the previous evening, wearing a bright orange tube that looked oddly out of place with a face so streaked and woebegone. She was very small and frail-looking, and seemed almost too young to be Kitchener's mother. She tugged with a thin hand at the loop of yellow beads that dangled right below her waist.

"I thought she'd be back," she said to Kitchener. "Where's your pa?"

"Gone up pier," he answered, "Fishing. And—" he hesitated, "—with you-know-who."

"Oh, I know *who*," she said, tossing her head. "And as for fishing, very nice, I'm sure. We shall enjoy a nice raw fish for our dinners."

"Uncle Sam'el'll cook it, ma," Kitchener said. "He said he would. Or we can go there and eat it."

"We shall do no such thing," she said. "I'm house-keeper here, thank you very much! House! Ten foot square, no chimney, windows papered up . . ."

"Look, ma, we're *lucky*. We could've had nowhere. We could easy've been sleeping *under* the pier. Cheer up, ma. It's no end of a lark, really."

"Lark? Lark?" Her voice rose and ended in a kind of despairing wail. For a moment Carrie thought she was going to burst into tears again. Instead, she determinedly re-ordered her face from a look of woe to one of something very like fierceness, and then looked straight at Carrie herself.

"How much does *she* know?" she asked.

"She still talks as if I'm not here," Carrie thought, piqued. "Does she think I'm deaf or dumb or something?"

"I don't know all that much," she replied herself. "All I really know is that you're from 1921—"

"What did you go and tell her that for?" Ellen turned on Kitchener and the yellow beads swung out in a wide arc.

"He didn't!" Carrie cried. "At least, not till I'd already guessed. I saw your photograph—I'd have known anyway!"

"What photograph?"

Now, at last, some kind of barrier had been broken down. Ellen was speaking directly to her. Silently Carrie pointed to the kiosk opposite and all three of them went over to it. Ellen regarded the picture in silence for a minute. Then she drew a deep sigh.

"You don't hardly know what's real," she said at last. "That—or this."

She turned away again.

"What else do you know?"

"That's all, really. Except about the Three Times Seven, and being invisible. And I even knew about that, in a way. I did it yesterday without even knowing."

Ellen turned and looked at her then—*really* looked at her, for the first time, as a real person.

"That's true," she said thoughtfully. "As if it was *meant*, almost. A person wouldn't hit on the Three Times Seven in a thousand years, not unless it was meant . . ."

For a moment her face softened, looked hopeful and almost glad, and Carrie, hesitantly, smiled back.

"You could be *good* luck, not bad. . . ." Ellen murmured.

"Course she is, ma! Look at Muff—he liked her, straight off. He'd have bit her if he didn't. And we're going to need help—you said so yourself. She'll help—won't you?"

"Yes, yes, of course I will!" Carrie cried.

"Not that I like begging favours," said Ellen grudgingly at last.

"It wouldn't be a favour," Carrie told her. "I'd like it. Truly, I'd love it. I mean, look at me now—invisible! I can hardly believe it!"

Ellen stared.

"You mean you *like* being invisible? Like it?"

"I love it!" Carrie cried. "It's magic!"

"Well I don't," said Ellen. "And if you'd had as much magic as I've had this last dozen years, you'd be sick to death of it, same as I am. I've no use for it at all, particular the kind *we* get. Half and half magic's no good to anybody. Look where it's got us. If ever I once get my feet back in 1921 where they belong, I shall have done with magic for the rest of my days. I wasn't brought up to it, and I don't like it."

Carrie could see that she had said the wrong thing.

"I might be Pontifex by name," Ellen went on, "but I ain't by nature, and never will be. Here's George now."

George was wearing a brightly striped blazer and a boater hat. He was swinging a basket and whistling with a fine disregard for the distracted gulls. He stopped whistling when he saw them looking, and began to frown and look serious. Carrie guessed that this was out of respect for Ellen's mood, and that the frown was only skin deep.

"Got a fish each," he announced, banging down the basket. "Morning, miss."

"Good morning," Carrie said.

"And one over for Muff. It's the jellies you've got to

watch for—real whoppers. Pity you can't eat 'em. There's enough jellies down there to feed us breakfast, dinner and supper all winter—and what a thought!"

"As far as I can see," said Ellen, "it makes no difference. I don't fancy eating a fish raw any more than I fancy eating a jelly."

"Come on, Ellen old girl," he said, putting an arm round her shoulders. "We shan't starve, you know, whatever you say."

"I shall!" she retorted. "I shall, rather than go eating at other folks's tables—strangers' tables. Strangers that I don't even like very much and can't even cook eggs. I'll starve, if need be."

"Jove!" cried George, giving Ellen's stiffened form a tight hug, "Jove, if you ain't a queer one. There's old Uncle Sam'el down the pier, takes us in and makes us welcome, puts a roof over our heads and food in our bellies, and she don't like him, and says he can't cook eggs. All right, old girl, if he can't cook eggs, we'll try him with fish!"

"I want to cook them!" cried Ellen passionately, struggling free from his embrace. "He shan't have them!"

"But Ellen," he said patiently, "we ain't got a stove."

"Then get one!" she cried. "If I'm to live here for ever and ever as it seems I am, thanks to the Pontifexes and their clever tricks, then I'll have a stove! And I'll have the house made proper and fit to live in, and curtains up at the windows. Oh oh—I think I shall go mad —I can't stand it! We haven't even got our own knives and forks! We haven't even got a water closet! Half a mile up pier every time we have to go! It's not human, and I can't stand it! And we shall be here for ever and ever, I know we shall!"

She turned and ran into the kiosk and slammed the door. The newspapers billowed and rippled in the draught. From inside came the sound of noisy sobbing. George looked apologetically towards Carrie.

"She's not Pier, you see," he explained. "Not true blue Pier, anyhow, poor old girl."

"Is it true, what she said?" Carrie asked. "Will you really be here for ever and ever?"

"Depends," he said.

"Depends on what?"

"What she means, partly. You see, to Ellen, for ever and ever is about a fortnight, by most people's time. And I reckon we *might* be here that long. Not that she exaggerates deliberate," he added hastily. "It's just that to Ellen, it'll *seem* like for ever and ever."

"She certainly seems upset," Carrie said. "Are you really all living in that kiosk?"

"It's all right," said Kitchener. "I like it. I've got a hammock."

"Ah, but you've got to look at it from your ma's point of view," said George. "She's house proud, she is, and it's hard on her. And she likes company, and a bit of fun. Tell the truth, it's not being out of time worries her. Oh no. Give her a nice, tidy little home and she couldn't care if she was in 1980, or 2080, for that matter. It's the being all at sixes and sevens that's got her down. She likes to have her pretty things round her. She can't settle."

"Rats!" murmured Kitchener under his breath.

"But can't you make it like home?" Carrie asked, rather to her own surprise. They both looked questioningly at her, so she was bound to go on.

"I mean, couldn't you get a little stove—one of those camping stoves, you can cook practically anything on them. And you can get crockery and things at Woolworth's and you could soon put some curtains up instead of all that newspaper—I don't think *my* mother'd like that, to tell you the truth. I mean, I don't see how *anyone* could settle somewhere with *newspapers* up at the windows. But you could make that kiosk really comfy, if you wanted to."

"Think so, do you?" said George at length.

"It'd be fun," said Carrie. "And it would take her mind off things. I'll help."

George looked at her intently.

"I don't think I quite caught your name," he said.

"It's Carrie, short for Caroline. We could make a list of all the things you needed, and then I could go and fetch them. Kitchener could perhaps come as well. He doesn't look so—" she broke off.

"Oh, I know what you're getting at," George said. "We can see for ourselves fashions have changed. Though come to that, nobody took no notice in London, nor yet on the train. The old man got a stare or two, but then he always does. You can see *he's* different, fashions or no fashions."

"London?" cried Carrie. "You've come from London? That's where I'm from. But I thought you were Pier people!"

"Oh, and so we are," agreed George. "Cockney Welsh, through and through. But when you get switched forward fifty years by accident, see, you can't choose when and where it'll happen. Nice if you could, but there you are. Got our own little digs in London, see, for winter. April to September Pier, October to March London. That's the way we do it."

"I still don't really see how you *got* here, though," said Carrie. "Can it really happen to anyone, then?"

"Oh, not to anyone," George said. "You'd only really find it happening to a Pontifex."

"We might as well tell her about Gamper straight off, pa," put in Kitchener. "She's going to find out, anyhow. How's he doing down there?"

"Fairish, I suppose," said George. "Bit bad-tempered. He's trying, though, I'll give him that. He'll be up at dinner for his fish."

Carrie listened to this exchange in bewilderment. There was really only one sense she could make of it.

"Do you mean there's *another* of you?" she cried.

"Grandfather," said George. "The Great Pontifex, Last of the Magicians. He's up pier, last on the left. It's draughty up there, I'll grant you, but he's used to that and he needs the quiet. Working out how to get us back, see."

"Last of the Magicians?" Carrie felt a delicious thrill run up her invisible spine. "Oh! Really a magician?"

"The last," said George. "Literally. It's a dying strain. Not an ounce of it left in me, and even Ponty's only got it in patches. That's the trouble, see. He's got the kind of magic'll fill a pier from top to bottom in high season—

oh, yes, he's got that, all right. But when it comes to the real stuff, the poor old boy's in the dark. No idea at all, really. I should never've thought he'd got it in him to do this much, to tell truth. It's real old time magic, you know, jumping fifty years, and it's shaken the old man up, I reckon. Surprised himself, if you ask me. Keeps trying to make out he never even *did* it. I should like to know who else, whatever!"

"You mean to say," said Carrie, "that there's a real magician, a real, live magician, up the pier?"

"What else have I been saying, this last five minutes?" said George. "I told you. The Great Pontifex himself. Last of the Magicians."

"Oh!" exclaimed Carrie softly. "Oh!"

In the silence they heard again the sound of muffled sobbing from inside the kiosk. George looked enquiringly at Carrie.

"Shall I have a word, then?" he asked. "About the stove, and whatnot?"

Still dazed, Carrie nodded. George went into the kiosk and gently closed the door behind him. Carrie looked at Kitchener.

"A real magician?" she asked again. She could not help herself—she had to hear it said again.

Kitchener stood stiffly up to attention and began to beat an imaginary drum.

"The Great Pontifex, the Last of the Magicians! Roll up and see him turn water to milk and milk to water. See butterflies big as cabbages conjured out of thin air! See a rabbit grow twenty times as large as life, and shrink no bigger than a pea! Roll up, roll up! Don't believe your eyes—it's all done by magic! And the World's most incredible sight—see the Great Pontifex vanish into thin air! No tricks, no strings—it's all magic! You'll see him come, you'll see him go, and it's sixpence adults and children a threepenny bit! Don't miss your chance, it's the last of a lifetime. It's the Great Pontifex, the Last of the Magicians."

He lowered his arms and looked at her.

"Believe it now?"

Carrie nodded. Kitchener grinned.

"You'll get over it," he told her. "Want a gob-stopper?"

Again she nodded. She seemed to have lost her voice. He handed over a violently coloured ball of toffee. She put it in her mouth and he fished out another and followed suit. Conversation, for the present, was at an end.

Chapter Six

By the time the kiosk door opened again the gob-stoppers were only a taste upon the tongue, and it was nearly twelve. Carrie stared at her wristwatch in disbelief—she had half imagined that invisibility went hand-in-hand with timelessness.

"We'll try it," George said firmly to Carrie. "We're going to try and settle in and make the best of things, ain't we, Ellen?"

Ellen nodded. She was still pale, but the tears had quite gone now, and when she spoke there was a new firmness in her voice.

"I've made a list," she said. "And George was saying you'd kindly shop for us."

"Oh, I will!" cried Carrie, delighted. "But I can't stop now, I'm afraid—I shall be late for dinner. If you tell me a few things and give me the money, I can get them on the way back this afternoon."

"Stove first," said Ellen firmly. "I shall save the fish, George, for supper. We'll go down to Sam'el's now and have a cold bite, and that'll be the last. Give her the money, George."

George handed Carrie a grubby canvas bag tied with drawstrings.

"Mostly silver," he said apologetically. "Takings, see."

"Four each cups, saucers, plates and side plates," went on Ellen. "And four each knives, forks, spoons, tea-spoons and a pair of tablespoons. Then I shall want—"

"Wait!" cried Carrie. "I'll never remember all that!"

"Give her the list, Ellen," advised George. "You can easy make another. There's a lot yet you've not thought of."

"That's true," agreed Ellen. She handed Carrie the paper. "You can get what you can, then, and we shall be most obliged. And don't go for cheapness, particular with the cutlery. I like a bone handle with my knives. And get something a bit pretty for the china, will you? Something colourful. And while I think—a breadknife. Give it back a minute, will you?"

Carrie handed back the list and looked again at her wristwatch.

"Come on, Ellen old girl," said George. "The child's got to be gone."

Ellen scribbled hastily and handed back the list and Carrie set off at a run, calling over her shoulder:

"Back by about three!"

"Don't forget the Three Times Seven when you come!" shouted Kitchener after her.

Then she was over the line and visible again, though feeling not a jot different for it, and once more the gulls were in commotion. They followed her to the pier gates and as she went through she caught a glimpse of the keeper in his doorway and half thought he shouted something after her. She could not wait to find out.

Dinner at Craig Lea seemed an oddly unreal affair to Carrie, quite apart from the general wateriness of its flavour. The problems that her mother and aunt discussed to and fro across the table seemed thin and trivial compared with those of the shipwrecked and marooned Pontifexes. Because that was what they were —marooned as surely on that pier fifty years away from home as any Robinson Crusoe on a desert island. Their problems were not to be solved by ordinary means. They had only the battered and wavering magic of an old magician, the last of his race, fumbling his spells and muttering half-forgotten chants down there at the pier's end above the distraction of the gulls and waves.

Carrie had hidden the list and the money bag in her room, and went straight up there after the meal was over.

"I think I'll lie down a bit before I go out," she told them. "I feel tired."

They had nodded approvingly over their cups of tea and returned to their conversation.

In her room Carrie took the bag from the drawer and flung herself on the bed. She pulled open the draw-strings and peered inside.

"There's pounds!" she realized, awed. She opened the list. It was written in a neat, copperplate writing, as if for an exercise.

Stove (must be very safe)
4 each cups, saucers, plates, side plates
4 each knives, forks, spoons, teaspoons
2 tablespoons
frying pan
kettle
2 saucepans (1 large, 1 small)
large mixing bowl
2 one-pint basins
2 bars scrubbing soap
scrubbing brush
breadknife
(Please turn over)

Carrie turned over.

salt, pepper, mustard
flour
sugar
lard
butter
potatoes, carrots, onions
dozen eggs
marmalade
pound best rashers
bananas
breast of lamb
gravy browning
mint humbugs

For several minutes she lay there overwhelmed by the enormity of her task.

"I can't carry all *them*," she thought. She stretched

out and crossed her hands behind her head, thinking hard.

The solution turned out to be a surprisingly simple one.

"I'll order the things and pay for them," she decided. "Then I'll take a few of the urgent things and have the rest delivered to the gatehouse. After all, Mr Pontifex is one of the family. He won't mind."

Next she sorted the heavier silver from the bag and changed it into pound notes from her own spending money. It would look queer if she paid the larger bills all in silver. The bag itself was likely to draw attention, so she put the pound notes and five pounds in silver into her own handbag. The rest she hid in a large cabin trunk containing her own books and toys, certain that no one would look in there. Just to be sure, she locked it and put the key in her handbag.

"Now I'll have to make sure I don't lose my handbag," she thought, and felt faintly dizzy at the mere idea. This was the third handbag she had had in a year. The others she had lost.

The shopping took nearly an hour and it was after three by the time Carrie reached the pier gates. She was carrying a carrier bag with the greengrocery in it and a bucket containing the cleaning things. The groceries were to be delivered later that afternoon. She had found a shop that sold camping equipment and bought a stove from there, as well as all the crockery and cutlery. She felt a little nervous about these items and wondered whether they would come up to Ellen's expectations.

She waited by the gate and after a minute old Samuel

Pontifex appeared. He was looking pleased with himself, and wiping his hands on a tea-towel that was tucked in at his waist as a makeshift apron.

"Just washing up," he told her. Then, in a lowered voice, "Had the family in to dinner, you know."

"Yes, they told me. It must be nice for you, finding your family again."

"Still hardly believe it," he said. "But I shall get used to it, I reckon. Right on the doorstep, too. Not a day'll pass but what I'll see 'em."

"It's a pity it's not for always," Carrie said. "You'll miss them when they've gone again."

"Might *be* for always," said the old man, looking up with bright eyes.

"I expect the Magician will get them back in the end. After all, he got them *here*."

"Aye, aye. So he did." He leaned forward. "You're not saying a word of this, are you? Not to anyone?"

"Of course not! As if I would!"

"Aye. well, that's all right, then. But you'll have to

watch you're not here overmuch. We don't want folk talking."

"Nobody sees me," she replied. "And nobody even knows I come here."

She told him then about the things she had ordered, and he listened intently.

"It's that wife of his that's put him up to this, of course," he said then. "They could've ate their meals here, I wanted 'em to. But she wouldn't have it, I could see that." He drew a great sigh. "It's always the same. It's a mistake, marrying out of Pier. A big mistake. They don't see things the same."

He looked like a kind of forlorn walrus with his drooping grey whiskers and mournful eyes.

"Never mind," she said. "I expect you'll see plenty of them while they are here. And perhaps you can go and have meals with them sometimes."

But even as she spoke she remembered that Ellen had ordered only four each of everything. There would be no invitations up the pier for the old man—unless he was expected to bring his own cutlery.

"After all, he is a sort of cousin," went on the gate-keeper.

"Who is?"

"Why, George, o' course."

"George? But he's—" she broke off. She was going to say, "But he's *years* younger than you are!" and then she remembered. George was still in 1921. If *he* were in 1971, then his whiskers too would be grey and his back stooped.

"What?" he was saying. "What?"

"Nothing. I was all mixed up for a minute. It is a bit complicated, isn't it?"

"Could be for some, I suppose. 'Tain't for me. But then, o' course, they're my family."

"Yes, they are," she agreed.

"Now if you was to have seen the Pier how it was in them days, that *was* complicated, if you like. I tell you, Pontifex from top to bottom, it was. One big family. Was to me, least, for I'd lost my parents, see. Queenie, she looked after me—a sort of an aunt, she was. Had the kiosk right at the end, telling cards and fortunes. Went in for crystal ball gazing, too, she did. You can't be a Pontifex and not have a streak of magic in you somewhere. Then there was Albert—he did conjuring and Punch and Judy, and then there was Maisie and Sidney —oh, you could go on all day. I should give anything to see it all again, as it was in the old days. 'Tain't the same now. Just ain't the same."

Carrie stood hesitating. She could tell that he would have liked to go on talking about the old days, and all his relations, but she herself was longing to be away and up the pier, pacing out the Three Times Seven and back in the invisible world of the squatters.

"I'll be getting along, then," she said. "The things shouldn't be too long. They said they'd send them straight away."

"Tell George he'll have to come down here to fetch 'em. I can't leave here, see. Not during Pier hours. Not that I'm likely to be missed, but there you are. Duty's duty."

"Oh, it is," she agreed. "I'll tell him."

Then she was away, running as usual, eager to reach the line that divided land from sea and, for her, the visible from the invisible. Then there were those few unsteady steps and she was back among them again, to the clockwork chorus of gulls, who showed not the least sign of becoming used to the optical illusions up the pier. But then gulls have never heard of optical illusions, so that was not surprising.

Chapter Seven

The kiosk door stood open and George was sitting outside, leaning his back against the wall.

"Is someone there?" came a voice from inside. "Shut the door, George."

"It's only the girl," George called. Ellen appeared, wearing a large apron over the orange tube and brushing a stray lock of yellow hair from her eyes.

"What've you got there?" she asked.

Carrie told her, and explained about the rest of the things.

"I thought you'd need the cleaning things first," she said.

"Ah!" Ellen was pleased. "You keep a sharp look out now, George, while I get scrubbed out. Kitchener's up pier," she added to Carrie. "Ponty wouldn't come down to Sam'el's for dinner, so Kitchener's taken him a bite up there. And if you're going up, ask him to bring some milk back, will you?"

She took the bucket and began unpacking it.

"And if you *are* going up there," added George,

"don't take too much notice of Ponty. I think he's got his Delusions of Grandeur on."

"Oh dear!" Carrie could not think what else to say, not being quite sure what Delusions of Grandeur were.

"Oh, it'll pass off," said George. "Always does. I just thought I'd mention it."

"Thank you. Yes, thank you."

As Carrie approached the last kiosk on the left she could see Muff ahead, wandering aimlessly, tail down, and wondered whether he were invisible or not. He looked bored, and doubtless was. Nobody ever seemed to come up the pier except herself and the Pontifexes, and he had probably given up all hope of ever coming across an exciting scent on the damp wooden boards.

"And perhaps we haven't even *got* scents," she thought. "Being invisible."

She saw a corner of the newspaper blinds being lifted and caught a glimpse of Kitchener before it dropped again. As she drew level with the half open door of the kiosk his voice called out:

"Come in! It's all right!"

She pushed the door a little wider, but stayed outside. Her eyes went straight to the figure seated on an up-turned box in the far corner. The light, filtered through paper, was dim and yellowish. The Last Magician sat motionless as an ivory yet intent, alert as a bird. To her relief there was no suggestion of grandeur, only of *difference*, an enormous, unmistakable difference from any other old man in the world who might be sitting quietly on a box, thinking. She tried to think what this difference could be, but could find no words for it. She

had noticed before that there are plenty of words for
likenesses, hardly any at all for differences.

She was certain it had nothing to do with his clothes,
though he wore a tall, cone-shaped hat such as you
would hardly expect to sit behind on the bus, and a

flowing yellow gown over what seemed to be an ordinary tweed suit with a watch chain dangling over the waistcoat. She noticed a whitish goatee beard, and long thin wrists poking from his sleeves and hands resting on what looked like very long, thin legs. He was a jumble of sharp, ill-adjusted angles, oddly double-jointed-looking.

"It's the girl, Gamper," Kitchener said, but made no attempt to reverse the introduction. Carrie smiled politely and made a little bow. The old gentleman glanced at her and then away again with a total lack of interest.

"Good afternoon. I'm honoured to meet you," she said.

No reply. Not even a second glance.

"I've just been doing some shopping," she offered.

In the silence that followed she saw with horrid clarity what a ridiculous remark this was to have made to the Last of the Magicians.

After what seemed a very long while Kitchener himself got up from the floor without a word and came outside. He jerked his head for Carrie to follow and wandered off towards the pavilion. Carrie looked again at the Great Pontifex and as she did so he closed his eyes, quite deliberately. She paused, half expecting to see them open again immediately in a kind of slow-motion blink. They remained closed, purposefully, as if he were offering up some kind of prayer—as well he might be, she supposed, under the circumstances.

"He doesn't say much, does he?" she said, catching up with Kitchener. "Is he always like that?"

"Only if he doesn't want to talk. You should hear him sometimes. Did he shut his eyes at you?"

Carrie nodded.

"That's it, then. Always does that if he don't want interrupting. Does it to us, sometimes."

Carrie was enchanted by the sheer lordliness of the gesture. It seemed such a sublime way of cutting people —simply to close one's eyes—the perfect dismissal. She imagined herself closing her eyes, slowly and deliberately, at certain people of her own acquaintance, and felt a delightful sense of power.

"Trouble is," Kitchener went on, "he's gone and overdone it this time, and he knows it. Not that he'll ever admit it, mind. Bet he didn't even know he'd got it in him to get us here, let alone get us back again. Keeps saying he never done it. Says he don't even remember making a spell. Says if he done it, he must've done it in his sleep."

"Could he have done?" asked Carrie.

Kitchener shrugged. They had reached the end of the pier and he leaned his arms on the rail and hung over, staring down at the greeny swell.

"*Could've*," he replied. "I *s'pose*. He was sure enough snoring away in the corner most of the way. They all were."

"Which corner? Who? When?"

"On the train," he replied. "That's when it happened, see. We set off from here on the train, and it's 1921, and we get to Paddington and it's 1971. Marvellous. All for the price of a ticket."

Fleetingly Carrie remembered the journey down, the

73

curious sense of a lull, a suspension in time and space, the rushing landscape and hypnotic iron song of the wheels, and she saw how easily it might have happened —even to herself. Perhaps after all the old man was right, and it was no spell of his making that had brought them here. Perhaps at a rare, given moment, time and space and motion could come together to work their own alchemy, distil their own magic.

"We could tell something was up, the minute we got there," Kitchener was saying. "You know—the way things looked—the engine was different, everything. We never even went out the station. Minute pa got a newspaper we saw what'd happened. So we caught the next train back."

"But how did you know the gatekeeper would turn out to be your uncle?" Carrie asked.

"Didn't. Got as big a shock as he did. But whoever it'd been, he'd have been Pier, see. So it didn't really matter."

"And is the Last of the Magicians really your grand-father?" she asked. "He looks older than anyone's grandfather I know."

"He's Pontifex and so're we," he replied. "So it don't really matter. There's hundreds of Pontifexes spread out here and there, up piers. You soon lose count of who's who. The ones on your pier, you count them as family, see. Like Uncle Sam'el. Bet he's not my uncle. But he was on our pier, before he ran off. What's it matter?"

"Oh, it doesn't," Carrie assured him. "I just won-dered, that's all."

She wondered, too, how many children she would

have to have when she grew up in order to start a family that would have so many ramifications that it lost count of itself. She made a swift guess at twenty or thirty and promised herself she'd work it out properly later, with pencil and paper.

To her disappointment, she saw no more of the last Magician that afternoon. He sat and wrestled alone with his wayward spells.

Later, she and Kitchener set off back down the pier to see how Ellen's homemaking was progressing. Between them they carried a can of milk that had been sea water only an hour earlier, brought up by dipping a bucket over the edge of the pier on a long piece of twine.

"I s'pose as long as he can still do his old tricks, there's hopes," Kitchener remarked. "But what if he can't pull it off, and we're here for ever?"

They looked sideways at one another.

"Would you mind very much?" Carrie asked at last. "At least you're still with your family. And you needn't stay invisible, once you'd settled in."

"But we'd have to stop up pier for ever!" he cried. "We couldn't even go back to London winters!"

"Why not?"

Kitchener stopped suddenly and a wave of milk rose and broke over the side of the jug.

"We've got no papers!" he cried. "You got to have papers, Uncle Sam'el says."

"What kind of papers?"

"Proper ones, official ones. To say who you are. He says you got to have 'em for everything, and you've got

75

to have papers saying when you were born and papers with your number on, you've got to have a number, and—" he threw out his arms and the milk flew again "—oh, I dunno! Papers for everything!"

Carrie was silent. She had already seen enough forms being filled in to know that what Kitchener said was probably true.

"You even have to fill one in at the *dentist*," she remembered.

"I don't fancy stopping half my life invisible," he was saying, "and that's what Uncle Sam'el wants us to do. He says we can stop here, and he'll see us safe. Just what he'd like, that is. Come visible in the summer, he says, and work up pier, then winter invisible, like we are now. He's mad, if you ask me."

Carrie said nothing.

"Besides," he added ruthlessly, "*he* won't last for ever. And what then?"

"That was a horrible thing to say," Carrie said, after a pause.

"Well? It's true, isn't it?"

"Perhaps it is. But you shouldn't *say* it."

"If things are true, I *say* them," he said obstinately. Then, as an afterthought, "*And* if they're not, sometimes. Everyone does. So you needn't pretend *you* don't."

They were coming close to having their first quarrel and Carrie was relieved to find that they had nearly reached the first kiosk and that George and Ellen were both there waiting.

George had been down to the gatehouse and collected

the deliveries, and Ellen was so pleased that she seemed almost a different person.

"Come and have a look," she invited, and Carrie, for the first time, entered the kiosk.

"Shut the door after you, George," she warned, as the others came in after her. "You know what Sam'el said. As long as we keep the door shut, there'll be nobody the wiser."

Carrie looked about her and made admiring remarks about Ellen's homemaking. Of course, the windows were still papered with newspaper, which gave the whole place a temporary, "we're not stopping long" kind of feeling, but apart from that, Ellen really had succeeded in making it look something like home. A hammock was slung overhead and several blankets were folded over boxes to form seats. More boxes served as tables, and over one of them Ellen had draped what looked like a fringed pink shawl, and the new cutlery and crockery were set neatly out on top. The saucepans hung on nails above the little stove. On the opposite wall hung two ukeleles.

"Who plays those?" Carrie asked.

"Me and pa," Kitchener told her. "It's our act."

"*Do* it for me!" she begged.

"Not *now*," he said. "Ma, can I go on shore?"

"No," she replied. "You cannot. I told you. Don't keep bothering me, will you? We're none of us going on shore, and that's the end of it."

"He'd be all right," Carrie said. "He could come with me. He doesn't really look all that unusual. No one'd notice."

"That ain't the point," returned Ellen. "He can go under the pier, I've told him that, though I ain't even sure that I like that. But not one foot does he set on land. And George says the same. Don't you, George?"

George, looking uncomfortable, agreed that he did say the same.

"Your ma's got a kind of a *feeling* about it," he explained. "And so've I, in a way. It ain't quite right, see? We don't *belong* here."

Ellen was pushing up her sleeves, her eyes fixed on the boxes of provisions.

"As long as we stop here," she went on, "we're safe—or safe enough. But the minute we set foot on dry land—" she paused—"that's different, that's all. There's no telling what might happen. Here we are, and here we stop. Least, till the old man lifts us out of it. And let's hope he won't be too long about that. It's all very well to say 'Make yourself at home', but we *ain't* at home, and no use pretending. We're only *half* home."

"We got the place right, but not the time," suggested George.

"That's just it," she agreed, and began washing the five fat fish. She went on talking almost absently, as if she had forgotten that the rest of them were there.

"I was shivering last night, lying and listening to them waves smacking underneath. I lay there all of a-shiver, and hardly a wink did I have before them blessed gulls set up at dawn. And you know why?"

She put down the knife and faced the others now. They stared at her expectantly.

"I'll tell you." She widened her eyes and said in a hoarse whisper, "On account of them *footsteps*!"

She spoke the words so dramatically, they were so unexpected, that Carrie herself felt the faintest of shivers run down her back. For a moment she imagined the pier at night, the thin mists rolling in and then the darkness, and all night long the noises of the tide, the incessant whisperings and conspiracies of the deep water under the slatted boards. She looked at Kitchener and saw him wide-eyed and taken aback.

"What footsteps?" he demanded at last, probably sounding braver than he felt, Carrie thought.

"Two nights we've been here," Ellen said, "and two nights I heard 'em. Footsteps, slow and sure, right by the door. And then they'd stop, and there'd be someone out there, listening. And then they'd start again, going up the pier, up to where the old man sleeps. Then, after a bit, I'd hear 'em, coming back, and ooh George, they was horrible footsteps, so slow they was! And then they'd go past and back down the pier and I'd lie there listening and waiting and—oh!" she broke off abruptly.

"I'm doing wrong to speak of it! Look at that child—scared half out of his wits. Take no notice—I'm a silly girl and must've imagined it all!"

"I'm not scared," said Kitchener.

"Oh no, old girl," said George. "You didn't imagine it."

"Didn't?"

He shook his head.

"*I* heard 'em, see."

There was a little silence.

"There's one thing," said Ellen at length, "we could *both've* imagined it."

George let out a roar of laughter and everyone else jumped.

"Ho!" he cried. "What a girl! Talks herself into hearing footsteps, and now she's talking herself out of it, and me as well! And we both heard 'em, large as life, and why not? *I* know who it is, and so do you!"

"Who?"

"Sam, o' course! Sam'el Pontifex, sure as day."

"But why? Why should he come creeping up pier at dead of night? He's a deep one, and I've always said so, but what does he want, pray?"

"Want?" echoed George. "He don't want anything, I don't suppose. Doing his rounds, you might say. His job."

"Are you sure?" she said slowly.

"Sure? I'm not *sure*," he admitted. "But it stands to sense, don't it? Who else would it be?"

"Yes, ma," chimed in Kitchener. "Who else?"

"Don't ask me," she said darkly. "But we ain't sure, so we don't know."

"Then we'll find out," said George. "Tonight," he winked at Carrie, "I shall open the door and look!"

Ellen let out a shriek.

"No! George! You shan't! Do you hear me? You shan't!"

"All right, old girl," he said, laughing. "I'll ask Sam'el."

"And don't you do that either," she said quickly. "I don't like him."

"Oh, that!" said George.

"Yes, that," she said flatly. "He's a thorough nasty, interfering old man, and worse, I shouldn't wonder. Gives me the creeps, sitting there in that room with his talking pictures and everlasting talk about Pontifexes and piers. Keeps talking about the old days—and old days they might be, to him! But it's *our* time he's talking about, and it thoroughly depresses me, him going on as if it was all over and done with. Old days indeed! Talking pictures!"

"He explained about that, Ellen," said George patiently. "Everyone's got talking pictures in their houses, he says. Television, it's called."

"Well, I don't like people that's strangers sitting in a room looking at me when I'm talking," she persisted.

"They can't see *you*, Ellen, and they can't hear you. They're just—they're just talking pictures. And as to his everlasting talk about piers and Pontifexes, why, it's only natural. Poor old fellow—he's like a dog with two tails to have us here, you can see that. Have a heart, Ellen. We're the first Pontifexes he's had sight of for fifty years and more. And when they get to his age, folk like to go on about the old days. You got to humour him a bit, Ellen."

"You're too soft, George," was all she said.

"Shall *I* ask him if he comes up pier nights?" asked Kitchener. "I don't mind."

"You do no such thing!" she told him sharply. "You keep out of it. *You* ain't heard no footsteps, have you?"

"No," he admitted.

81

"Well, then. And nor've your pa and me, truth be told. You can hear anything, if you try hard enough, specially in the dark. And stuck out on a pier, I daresay you could hear 'em in broad daylight, if you listened hard enough. I daresay I could imagine I heard 'em right now!"

She paused and cocked her head, and in the silence, quite clearly, Carrie *did* hear footsteps. She let out a little scream and her hand flew to her mouth. All four of them stood there staring into each other's eyes as if to read confirmation there.

Outside the kiosk the footsteps halted. Ellen too had her hands over her mouth now. Carrie began furiously counting the narrow boards of the wall opposite. The footsteps started up again, going up pier.

"Quick!" Ellen hissed. "Look under the blinds, George!"

Swiftly he stooped and lifted one of the sheets of newspaper, and the others crowded behind him. His shoulders began to shake, he let the paper fall.

"Look!" he managed to splutter.

Carrie pushed her head beside the others' and looked. An elderly gentleman, hands clasped behind his back, was sauntering casually up the pier, looking about him. Whoever he was, he clearly belonged to 1971, and just as clearly was taking a quiet, innocent afternoon stroll up pier.

"There you are, then!" cried Ellen. "What did I tell you? You can imagine anything!"

And so the matter dropped. Carrie herself did not like to point out the fatal flaw in Ellen's argument.

Those footsteps, the ones they had all just heard, had not been imaginary. They had been real. And so who could say whether the other ones, the ones in the night, were not real too?

Chapter Eight

Next day Carrie could not go to the pier at all. Her mother and aunt had decided that she should have a treat, and broke the news to her that evening. It was to be an outing to a castle some thirty miles away. They were to take a picnic lunch and have the whole day out. She saw at once that it would be a terrible day and there was no way out of it.

It would not have been so bad, she thought angrily, as she undressed for bed, if they hadn't made it a *surprise* treat. At the best of times, she hated surprise treats. They were on you before you had even time to think about them, let alone dwell on them, imagine the details and make the necessary preparations. And this particular surprise treat was more like a clap of doom.

In bed she tossed restlessly. There was not a chance that she could let the Pontifexes know what had happened. She had been going to do their shopping for them, and they would think that she had abandoned them. Worse, they might even think she had betrayed them, and spend the day barricaded in their tiny kiosk waiting for the heavy tread of footsteps and a loud knocking on the door. Worse still, perhaps the Last of the Magicians, sorting the ravel of his mixed spells at the end of the pier, would suddenly pull out the right thread, and when Carrie returned they would be gone for ever, magicked away in the night.

She lay for so long turning over her problems that she heard the others climbing the stairs to bed, and long after that, even, she could not sleep. At last she threw back the covers and got up. She went to the window and looked out to see the roofs and walls of the town below gleaming yellowy-grey in the light of the street lamps. She strained her eyes in the direction of the pier and thought she could just make out the little gatehouse with a light burning in an upper window. But the darkness drank the distances up, swallowed outlines and edges, so that it might have been the light of a ship she saw, far out at sea.

Another light caught her eye, no more than a prick but seeming to bob and dance, and she remembered Ellen's story of the footsteps. Was someone walking the quiet pier at this very moment, carving a path with a flashlight over the deck? She pictured the Pontifexes crouching there in the darkness over the waves and suddenly dropped the curtain and was back in bed, the covers up to her ears. When at last the thudding of her heart had quietened she thought, "I'll get up early in the morning. That's what I'll do. Before breakfast. I'll go down and tell them." Then she fell asleep and was woken by the voice of her mother by her bed, telling her to come to breakfast. In the very instant of waking

Carrie remembered her resolve, and the day was spoilt before it had even begun.

It was a terrible day. To begin with, there was a letter from her father. Carrie stared at the familiar handwriting, at least proof of his *existence*, before taking the envelope in to her mother. Carrie watched her face as she read it, frowning and puckering up her lips. Then she saw that Aunt Ester was watching, too, curiously, like a kind of eavesdropper. Carrie ran back up to her

room, where she heard their voices floating up from the basement, and then the sound of her mother crying.

The castle was closed for the winter, so all they could do was walk aimlessly around it and then spin out the picnic till it was time to catch the 'bus back. It was not even a proper picnic, just a cold, uncomfortable lunch sitting on a bench between her mother and Aunt Ester, who kept remarking brightly how pretty the leaves were at this time of year. Carrie crunched her crisps noisily to drown their conversation.

By half past nine the next day Carrie was out and running down towards the sea with the joy of an escaped prisoner.

"You again, is it?" remarked Sam'el Pontifex, sour and miserable and *pickled*-looking in the low sunlight. Carrie waved her ticket at him and waited impatiently for him to release the turnstile.

Down the first stretch, then the deck, now the Three Times Seven, and she was there! The door of the kiosk was closed. There was not a sign of the Pontifexes.

"Hello!" she called. "Kitchener! It's me!"

There was no reply. She stared at the blank, news-papered windows and felt in her bones that there was no one there. She went forward and knocked at the door.

"It's me! Carrie!"

Over her head the gulls went carelessly crossing paths, dropping out of the pearly sky in random ease, and suddenly Carrie's uneasiness became a sharp alarm and she cried aloud:

"The gulls! What's happened?"

When she had crossed the impossible line on the twenty-first board and vanished into thin air, there had been no furious clamour overhead, none of the usual protest from the cheated gulls. They were behaving exactly like any other gulls in the world, busy about their morning business, maddeningly carefree.

Carrie ran back over the edge of the deck, undoing

the magic of the Three Times Seven, and stared hopefully up at the gulls again. Not a sign—not a dip of a wing, an interrupted dive, or the least hint that the gulls cared a fig for anything but the fish and the weather.

"I must have got it wrong," she thought, though she knew she had not. She had paced those ritual steps with ritual care, despite her urgency. "I'll do it again."

The ball of her foot went on to the third plank, "two, three, four, five, six, seven!"

The kiosk stayed shuttered and silent. The gulls were dumb. She ran back yet again to the starting point. Still the morning went on, indifferent as ever.

Carrie stood fixed by fury and disappointment. She stamped her foot so hard that it hurt, and then was more furious than ever, and began to sob. The adventure that had hardly yet begun was already over. Her slender hold on the errant Pontifexes had been snapped by a single day out of their orbit.

"Hey, Carrie!"

She looked up. Blinded and dazed by tears she still knew that before her was Kitchener and that above her the gulls were rioting again, and that magic had happened.

"Come on," said Kitchener. "It's all right. You're making a horrible noise."

"I thought you'd gone!"

"No such luck," he said gloomily. "That'll be the day. Where did *you* get to yesterday?"

Carrie wiped her eyes on her sleeve and prepared to forgive him.

"I had to go out, I couldn't help it! I wanted to tell you but I didn't have a chance. But what's happened? I did the Three Times Seven, I did it twice, but it didn't work. Why didn't it?"

He grinned.

"Thought you knew it all, didn't you? There's more to magic than that. There ain't a Three Times Seven any more. It's *Seven* Times Seven."

She stared at him.

"We changed it, see? Safer."

It was as if he had slammed a door in her face. He went on hastily:

"Wasn't that we didn't trust you. But we didn't know what was up when you didn't turn up. You said you would, see, and then you didn't. How was we to know? And ma was in a terrible flap. It was her made Gamper change it. Anyhow, the first time you did it, you did it without even knowing, so *anyone* might've done, see? Wasn't safe."

Slowly Carrie nodded.

"I suppose not."

"Want to come, then?" he invited.

She nodded again.

"Right, then. Seven times seven, remember. It's a bit of a stretch, so easy does it. Three times it took me to get it right yesterday. Shouldn't like to have to do it in a hurry!"

They went tiptoe, arms spread wide like wings, taking long, wavering strides. To Carrie it seemed like a long journey and when at last she looked up to see George and Ellen watching her from the doorway of the kiosk, she felt as if she had travelled a long way to meet them.

"We heard what you was saying to Kitchener," began George awkwardly. "But you can see how we were placed."

"We weren't to know," Ellen put in.

"No, of course not." Carrie was so delighted to be back among them that she was ready to forgive them anything. "Did you manage all right?"

"Oh, we managed," replied Ellen. "Though I don't like asking favours of Sam'el."

"He don't mind, old girl," George told her. "I keep telling you."

"*He* don't mind," she replied tersely. "I do."

George winked at Carrie. She rather wished that he would not do this so often. It put her in a difficult position. She could not wink back—she didn't know how. At one time she had spent hours practising before a mirror, but in the end had given up. Her attempts at winks merely made her look as if she had a particularly painful headache. Because she could not wink, she usually felt she had to smile at him, and she did not like to do that, because it seemed to make a kind of conspiracy against Ellen. On this occasion, she looked away and pretended that she had not seen.

"I can do your shopping for you today," she offered.

Ellen smiled, looking all at once very young and pretty with her fair bobbed hair and little white teeth. Today she was wearing a lime green tube with a matching bandeau round her head, and the same long yellow rope of beads.

"I've made a list," she confided, "just in case, you know. We did think you'd turn up really, didn't we, George?"

"Oh yes," he agreed, flashing his teeth in turn. "We knew *you* were a pluck 'un."

"I'd never let you down," said Carrie. "Never."

The moment she had said it she felt a little silly, but was glad all the same, when she saw their faces. After all, she was a stranger still, and from another time, and they had only her own word that she would not betray them.

"How is the Last of the Magicians?" she asked then.

Ellen gave an impatient sniff and shrug, and George's bright face darkened.

"Gone broody, I reckon," he said. "Can't make the old man out at all, since we've been here. Seems to have lost all heart. Keeps saying the magic's gone out of him."

"It can't," said Ellen with decision. "Not now. He's *got to get us back!*"

Her small face was white and bleak.

"I know. I know, old girl," George said. "Don't you worry. He will, It's just another of his moods."

"He keeps saying sea water's got into his spells," put in Kitchener. "Could've, I suppose. He says they don't do what they're supposed to do. But that could be *him*."

"I expect it's just a passing phase," said Carrie after a small silence. Her mother often said this to comfort people. Unfortunately, on this occasion, nobody looked particularly comforted. The Pontifexes just looked at one another as if trying to read thoughts.

"I'll never forgive the old man if he don't get us out of this," said Ellen at last. "Never."

George looked uncomfortable, glanced towards Carrie as if to try a half-hearted wink, thought better of it, stuck his hands in the pockets of his gaudy blazer and began to whistle.

"And stop that!" cried Ellen, turning on him with a force that sent the yellow beads spinning in a wide arc about her. "You're too bad, George Pontifex! You never take *anything* serious. Never. If I was to turn into a blessed bird and take off this very minute, you'd do no more than stand with your hands in your pockets whistling!"

"Now, old girl," said George, removing his hands as if they had been burned, "you *know* I would."

"I know no such thing! Why don't you *do* something, instead of just standing about whistling and catching fish? *You* do something!"

George gazed helplessly round at the blank horizon as if looking for clues.

"What?" he asked helplessly at last. "What?"

"*I* don't know! Think of something! If we got here, there must be a way back, mustn't there? And I'm not stopping here, I'm not! I'm not cut out for this sort of thing, George, and that's the truth! I've tried to see the pleasure in it, and I absolutely can't. And to be stuck up a pier—that's the worst of the whole thing. Up a pier for ever and ever, with one mad old man one end and another the other, and—oh, I can't bear it, George, I can't!"

She did burst into tears now and ran to George who

held her against his blazer and kept giving her big, awkward hugs and gazed miserably over her bright head at Kitchener and Carrie.

"There, there, old girl," he said. "Don't you cry. George'll get you back home, I promise you."

"Oh George!" she lifted a tear-marked face. "George, will you?"

"Course I will," he affirmed.

"Oh George!" She gazed up at him with such admiration and affection that Carrie could hardly bear to watch.

"So let's hear no more about it then, shall we," went on the hero, producing a loudly coloured handkerchief that was immediately snatched and made use of.

"Come on, Carrie," muttered Kitchener. "Let's go up pier."

Eagerly she agreed. Family scenes were embarrassing enough even when they were one's own.

"Poor Ellen," she said as they set off, feeling that she should say something about the scene that had just passed.

"Poor nothing!" replied Kitchener.

"But she was upset—she was crying—she—"

"Rats!" said Kitchener.

Carrie was silent.

"It's just *her*," he said by way of explanation after a time. "You'll find out."

Again Carrie said nothing. After all, other people's mothers were their own affair.

"Anyhow," he went on, "how does she think *I* feel?"

"Oh Kitchener!" Carrie cried. "I know! It must be awful! I *do* know how you feel, I do honestly!"

"At least she's *had* half her life," he continued resentfully. "It wouldn't matter so much for her and pa. And as for Ponty, he don't care two pins. He could shift a thousand years forward *or* backward and all he'd do'd be blink. It's *me* that matters."

He went and stood leaning over the rail, staring out to sea. The birds went curling over the estuary in their wide, watery world of sky and sea.

"Just think," he said at length, in a very thin voice. "I'm sixty-one. Sixty-one years old! I'm an old man!"

"Oh Kitchener!" Carrie started to laugh, she could not help herself. "You don't look it!"

He turned on her then, furiously.

"Shut it! D'ye hear me? Shut it!"

Abruptly she closed her mouth. She stared at him, hardly recognizing him in his fury.

"You wait! I'll tell Ponty. I'll get him to spell you. I'll get him to turn you into something really horrible. Really horrible! You wait!"

She stared at him, aghast.

"I'm sorry! I'm sorry, Kitchener!"

He turned away again.

"So you ought to be. Just you look out, that's all."

He hunched over the rail.

"I didn't mean to laugh. And I'd do anything to help you. It was just that—oh well, I've *said* I'm sorry."

"All right," he said, without turning round. She stared at his back, trying to interpret it. She felt less sure of him than when they were face to face.

"Kitchener?"

"Yes?"—after a long pause.

"You wouldn't—you wouldn't *really* get the Magician to put a spell on me? Not really. Would you?"

Silence.

"Kitchener?"

No reply. Then she saw that his shoulders were moving, ever so slightly.

"Beast!" she cried, and hung out over the rail next to him to look into his face and find it creased and crimson with suppressed laughter.

Her terror of unbridled magic vanished. She let loose her own mirth, because she still wanted to laugh at the thought of Kitchener, sixty-one years old and not looking a day over twelve. She was ready, when he was, to go up the pier.

Interlude

The Last of the Magicians was remembering that his real name was Alfred. This was something that he found himself remembering more and more, these days. It was not even as if it were something he *wanted* to remember. But it kept floating up to the top of his mind despite himself, from time to time, from spell to spell, from wave to wave. Time, spells and waves all ran together in his head now, so that he could hardly separate them. Time, spells, waves. Time, spells, waves. . . .

"Alfred," he murmured aloud. "Alfred."

Now that he had actually spoken the name, it seemed to mean a little more. Even so, it still had an unfamiliar ring such as one would hardly expect one's own name to have. He could not even remember when anyone had ever called him by it. He tried hard to recollect, but failed. He had been the Great Pontifex, the Last of the Magicians, for too many centuries of spells and waves.

"Someone must have called me Alfred *some time*," he thought. Surely a baby in his cradle could not have been called The Great Pontifex? But then Alfred did not seem a very likely name for a baby, either. If it came to

97

that, it seemed unlikely that he had ever *been* a baby, though he supposed he must have been, once.

"What is really the matter," thought the Last of the Magicians, drawing a great sigh, "is that I am growing tired of being a Magician. I think I am running out of spells."

He went on musing, staring right ahead as he always did when he was thinking.

"It would be pleasant to be called Alfred," he thought. "I'd like that. Yes, I would."

He went on thinking.

"If my name were Alfred," he thought, "instead of The Great Pontifex, I would not be sitting all alone up pier, shut up like a clam. I would be down pier with the others, and even enjoying myself, I daresay."

He allowed himself to feel wistful for a moment. Then his eye fell on his magician's hat and he suddenly seized it and clapped it fiercely on his head.

"You are the Last Magician," he reminded himself. "There's spelling to be done, and only you to do it."

"A pity—what a pity," said the other voice in his head—the Alfred voice. But he pretended not to have heard it.

"They want to get back to their own time," thought the Last Magician, "though why I don't know. If they had lived for as long as I have, they would know by now that one time is really much the same as another. I really don't care *what* time I'm in, as long as I have my waves and spells."

"Even if they are wearing a little thin," put in Alfred.

"But I got them into this fix," went on the Great

Pontifex, ignoring the interruption, "or at least, so they say. And so I suppose it is my duty to get them out of it. And so I would, if I could."

"Would if you could, would if you could," said Alfred.

The Great Pontifex planted his knees wide apart and set a hand on each knee, in spelling position.

"Would if you could, would if you could, would if you could . . ."

Desperately he cast round his mind for a spell, but there seemed only room in his head for one voice at a time, and at present that one was Alfred's.

"Would if you could, would if you could, would if you could. . . ."

It was maddening. The Last of the Magicians was beginning to dislike Alfred so thoroughly that it was difficult to remember that Alfred was in fact himself—or part of himself.

"Oh be quiet!" shouted the Great Pontifex rudely at last, and he got up and began sorting through his bottles.

Even this gave him no pleasure today. He had been feeling less and less fond of his bottles, lately. They were refusing to work for him, and his affection for them was beginning to wane. He stared at them, row upon row of beautiful, ballooning glass, that was unlike any other glass in the world because it was more secret, more absolutely silent and containing. It held magic.

Even the magic was becoming daily more mysterious, because the Last of the Magicians was finding that less and less would it obey his wishes. It was almost as if those pale, watery essences were taking on a power of their own, going their own way. They were becoming strangers to him.

Admittedly, most of them had been mixed a very long time ago. Perhaps a century ago, perhaps two, who could say? The Last of the Magicians certainly could not. Nor could he remember what had gone into the making of most of them.

He stared at a flagon that was nearly empty now, with barely a few drops left at the bottom. Soon it would run out, and what then? He shut his eyes and tried to remember what had gone into the making of it. He let his mind drift, drift. . . .

Memory began to stir, moving like weeds on the sea bed. Pictures began to float up. It had been a hot day, when he had made that spell. He could feel the heat now, thick and powerful. His ears filled with the drone of bees and his long nose twitched at the remembrance of sharp and bitter smells. Nettles and nettleflowers, hyssop and—what was that?—rootweed, and a suddenly cold and pungent odour of roots deep dug and then the picture faded and another floated up in its place. Now it was the time of the spellmaking, the capture of essences, the distillation. All of it, all of it he remembered now, a century later, sitting in the cold, wind-crossed kiosk, eyes shut and sighing with pleasure now.

He opened his eyes and looked again at the near-empty flask.

"I have you now, my beauty," he said softly. "I could make you again, if I tried."

Now his gaze was fond again. After all, if the emptying flagons held secrets, they were secrets he had shared and still held, in deep-down recesses of his memory.

"I have let things slip," he told himself. "Perhaps I have been dabbling too much, living on summer piers and playing with half-magic. Rabbits out of hats and flowers from thin air, just to hear the crowds gasp. Not real magician's work at all. . . . How long since last I made a new spell?"

He could not remember.

"I shall *make* a new spell." His long back straightened, he placed his hands on his knees again.

"It'll be hard work."

It was Alfred again. This time the Last of the Magicians did not ignore him. He gathered himself up, savouring his loneliness at the draughty pier's end and feeling a new power run through his veins.

"Hard work, Alfred," he agreed. "No use at all to deny that. Very hard work indeed. Are you going to help me? Or shall I do it all by myself?"

He waited and listened. There was no reply. The Last of the Magicians smiled.

"Goodbye, Alfred," he said.

Chapter Nine

"Two weeks," thought Carrie. "Two weeks, we've been here."

This was as long as they had been supposed to stay, but no one had said anything about their going home. With a familiar, rising panic, she remembered again that they had no home. Their home had been sold, was lived in now by strangers. She thought of the Pontifexes in their kiosk and for a moment envied them, because at least they were all together, and so even the pier was a kind of home to them.

There was another letter from her father that morning. Carrie took it in to her mother and went straight back up to her room to tidy and make her bed. On the way out her mother stopped her and, surprisingly, hugged her hard.

"Where are you off to, darling?" she asked.

"Oh, just out."

"Poor little pet." Her mother hugged her again. "It's lonely for you here, I know. And you've been so good. It won't be long now, I promise you."

"Daddy!" cried Carrie, flooded with sudden joy. "Is Daddy coming? Has he found somewhere?"

Her mother drew away, but she was smiling.

"Just wait and see."

Carrie turned away, blinded with tears of rage and disappointment. As she opened the door she heard her mother's voice calling after her:

"Carrie, wait! What is it?"

But she did not wait.

"She'll have forgotten all about it by dinner-time," she thought.

When she reached the gatehouse Samuel Pontifex came out looking unusually pleased with himself. He looked, in fact, happy. Carrie was bound to notice so great a change, such an extraordinary absence of droop that altered his whole face and made him, for a moment, unrecognizable, as if Llangolly Pier had found itself a new keeper overnight.

A moment later she was wondering whether she had imagined it—whether the new face had been an optical illusion, a trick of the October light, a Welsh mirage. He saw Carrie and frowned. His whole face instantly rearranged itself into its familiar pattern—everyday Samuel Pontifex, pickled, sad, suspicious.

"You again?" he said. "Every blessed day. Haven't you got a home of your own?"

"No," said Carrie. "Not what you'd really call a home."

She felt for her season ticket in her pocket. After all, she had paid for it. She had a right to go on the pier whether the gatekeeper welcomed her or not. He took his time unlocking the wicket gate reserved for ticket holders, grumbling under his breath as he did so. She

thought she caught one phrase, "Blessed fly in the oint-
ment."

"Thank you very much," she said, and started up the
pier.

She supposed he was ill-tempered because he felt out
of things. He thought he had at last found himself some
kind of family, after fifty years of watching other fami-
lies go up and down his pier in holiday mood, and now
perhaps things were not turning out as he had expected.
None of the other Pontifexes had been exactly over-
joyed at the reunion, and Ellen positively disliked him.
They had shut him out of their world, and instead were
confiding in Carrie herself.

"But you can't *make* people like you," she thought.

Then she was deep in concentration, working the
tricky Seven Times Seven, and next minute, deafened
by a swarm of baffled gulls, was through the invisible
barrier into invisibility.

The Pontifexes stood in a little expectant huddle by
the kiosk, just as they had done that first day. She saw at
once that something was wrong.

"What is it?" she cried. "What's the matter?"

Her thoughts flew straight to the old magician at the
pier's end.

"The moon," said Kitchener bitterly then. "That's
what's the matter."

"The *moon?*"

"Near at the full. Three more days, and it will be full,
and then we're done. Done for good and all!"

Carrie looked at the others and read confirmation in
their grim faces.

"But why? I don't understand!"

"Ponty's been looking up his spells," Ellen told her. "Can't *remember* 'em, of course—can't remember anything. And now," her voice began to rise, "*now* he finds he's to get us out by the full moon, or we're here for ever. Oh George—for ever!"

Carrie, staring at her stricken face, was torn between shared terror at their plight, and dismay that soon— sooner than she had dreamed—she might lose them for ever, beyond all hope of recall.

"It can't happen, it *can't*!" burst out Kitchener, freckles burning. "Stuck invisible up a pier for the rest of our whole lives!"

"And with *him* at the other end, spying and creeping!" Ellen shuddered.

"*He* don't care!" said Kitchener. "You should've seen his face when I told him. Like a cat with a kipper. *He* don't care."

"No good taking it out on Sam'el," said George. "'Tain't his fault."

"He n-needn't be so p-pleased about it," cried Ellen, blowing her nose.

Carrie remembered the expression she had glimpsed on the pier keeper's face that morning. She had not imagined it, after all. Samuel Pontifex thought he had a family for keeps now.

"Ponty'll get us out," said George.

"I don't believe any such thing!" Ellen cried. "You heard what he said last night—he don't even know how he *got* us here, let alone how to get us back. Would you believe it? Do a trick like this, and not even to know how he's done it!"

"*If* he done it—did it," said George. "He ain't at all sure about that, Ellen, and no more am I. Keeps going on about *wishing*—says we must've been *wished* here."

"Wishing won't get us back!" flashed Ellen. "That *is* for certain, George Pontifex. *I've* wished, heaven knows, times and again, lying there in the dark night after night waiting for them horrible footsteps coming past the door!"

"Not *just* wishing, Ellen," said George patiently. "We all know that. There's magic wanted—and strong magic. But it's plain what Gamper says is true. He couldn't have magicked us here by accident, not unless he'd *wished* it—or someone else did."

"Wish *wash!*" said Ellen flatly. "I don't believe a word of what he says. He's gone to seed."

Carrie had a swift picture of spells flying in the salt air like seeds or thistledown, and shivered. Over Kitchener's shoulder she saw a steamer out beyond the headland, and clutched at its solid, painted shape like a straw, assuring her of her own place in time.

"At least *I'm* safe," she found herself thinking treacherously.

Ellen had sat down on an upturned crate at the door of the kiosk, pulling her woollen coat about her for warmth. She was staring over Carrie's own shoulder towards land, but her eyes were far away, as if she weren't really seeing it at all.

"Because it isn't real," Carrie thought. "Not for *her*."

"When I was little," said Ellen absently, "I used to

think a lot about magic. Witches and broomsticks, spells at the full moon—all of that. I'd lie awake in the dark and think and think about it. And I didn't but half know if I believed in it or not. But I always ended up thinking one thing, and that's what'd send me to sleep in the end. I always ended up thinking, 'Magic or no magic—it could never happen to me'."

There was a silence.

"Do you see what I mean?" she said.

"I can't imagine *not* getting back," said Kitchener slowly, "if that's what you mean. It just don't seem possible."

"There you are, then!" cried Carrie triumphantly. "It *can't* happen to you!"

"Well, we shall have to see," said Ellen grudgingly. But she looked brighter now and rose, smoothing her yellow tube. It almost seemed as if the matter were closed.

"But I should give anything, anything, just for half a minute back home again," she said. "Just half a minute, to be sure it's all still there."

"Still *there?*" Kitchener was alarmed again. "What d'ye mean, still there? Course it is! Only two weeks since we left, ain't it?"

"Might have seemed like two weeks to us," Ellen said. "But some people'd say it was fifty years ago. *She* would," nodding her head towards Carrie.

"Would you?" Kitchener turned on Carrie now, his face white. "*D'you* think 1921's still there?"

"I–I wasn't even born then," stammered Carrie.

"Wasn't even *born?*" he cried, horrified. "How can

107

—how can you—oh, *I* don't know! I'm fed up. Fed up! I hate this pier, I hate it! And if ever we do get back, I'll tell you one thing. I'm getting out of Pier, minute I'm old enough. Get a job ashore. I ain't spending my whole life stuck on *any* pier, now or never!"

With this he whirled and began to run down the pier towards land, Muff close at his heels. Carrie made to go after him but George put a hand on her arm.

"Best leave him. Upset. We all are."

"Temper, more like," retorted Ellen. She was almost herself again now. "Colour of his hair. My pa was the same. My luck, to get landed with red hair in my own family!"

"I think I'll get back anyway," Carrie said. "If you tell me what you want, I'll do some shopping, and then come back this afternoon."

Ellen nodded and smiled at her.

"We should hardly manage without you," she said. "Should we, George?"

George agreed that they shouldn't. A list was made and Carrie started back down the pier, planning her morning, wondering whether there was still time to catch up with Kitchener.

She looked ahead and saw approaching, heads bent against a stiff breeze, Aunt Ester and her mother. For a moment she stood frozen, staring like a dazzled rabbit. For an instant she remembered "I'm invisible!" but instinct was too strong. She turned and bolted back to the photograph kiosk, seeing from the corner of her eye the Pontifexes still leaning against their own door. Carrie crouched panting against the damp wooden walls, suddenly very close to the sea, sucking and slapping right beneath her. It seemed hours before she heard footsteps and then her mother's voice, though she could not catch the words, blown backwards as they were towards land by the onshore wind.

Carrie, clenched, stared down at the waves beneath the slats, willing the Pontifexes' invisibility to be intact, stunned by the unexpected head-on clash of her two worlds.

"I could get up," she kept telling herself. "I could get up and walk straight past them. They couldn't see me—I'm invisible."

And yet she dared not. If, perhaps, they had been strangers, she might have taken the plunge—put her invisibility to the test, risked meeting their eyes. But this was her own mother, and that she could not be seen by her was unthinkable, impossible.

She stayed until she was sure they must be safely past. Cautiously she edged round the corner and saw them, right beyond the second pair of kiosks now, close together, heads still bent. Slowly she straightened, her knees aching, and went back round the kiosk. The Pontifexes had disappeared, their door was shut.

"It's cold for them out here," Carrie thought. Almost she was tempted to knock at the door, reassure herself that they were still there, and she herself still in their world. But she did not.

"Of course they are," she told herself, and made back towards land, urged on by the wind.

There was no sign of Samuel Pontifex at the gatehouse and no sign of Kitchener, either. Carrie guessed

that he was under the pier, and decided to leave him.

As she set up the steep road towards the little square
the whole world seemed more than usually real and
now. The Pontifexes had lost their world, and for a
fraction of a minute back there on the gusty pier she had
caught a glimpse of what it must be to be anchorless in
time and place. She was passing a fishmonger's slab, and

stared at the slumped crabs, savouring the wet tang of their sea-soaked shells, *feeling* the horniness of their backs without even laying a finger on them. Beside them lay silver-backed and lovely mackerel, blindingly bright in the sun. She walked on, the ground beautifully solid under her feet.

She spent nearly an hour shopping, knowing there would be no one in the house if she went back to Craig Lea. When she had finished, she wandered round Woolworths, which reminded her of home because the smell and the feel of it was just the same as that of the Woolworths she had always known. She lingered longest, as always, over the jewellery. She caught sight of a string of yellow beads exactly—or nearly exactly—the same as the ones Ellen wore. And these were real, absolutely and certainly real, and only nineteen pence the string at that.

When she reached Craig Lea she hesitated at the foot of the steps, seized by the usual reluctance to go inside into the high dark hall with its closed doors and queer, fusty, antiseptic smell. But once she was inside, even that seemed oddly more real and friendly—familiar, like a real home. She ran up to her room, suddenly light-hearted.

Straight after dinner she went back to the pier, wearing her mac with its sou'wester stuffed into the pocket.

"Looks like a storm blowing up," Aunt Ester had said. "You can tell the signs. Your mother and I walked up pier this morning, and there was that kind of a feel about it."

"You wouldn't rather go to the pictures, would you,

dear?" her mother had asked. "We could easily put off what we were going to do."

"No harm in a drop of rain," Aunt Ester had said, and Carrie had shaken her head. She could hardly imagine a film that had ever been made that would compensate for an afternoon lost up the pier.

The gatekeeper seemed in better humour now, and let her through with no comment apart from "Storm coming up!" and a jerk of his head seaward.

The gulls, too, had sensed the storm, and were making small, uneasy rings, tossed by the same ragged gusts that flattened Carrie's mac against her legs and filled her mouth and lungs with air so cold that she could hardly breathe. Her seven by seven passed almost unnoticed by the distracted gulls.

The Pontifexes themselves seemed to have relapsed again into gloom. They were sitting inside the dim kiosk with the remains of a meal still lying around them, and Kitchener aimlessly strumming his ukelele.

They looked up and greeted her and she found herself a box to sit on. It was even darker than usual behind the newspapered windows, though the rising storm gave the room a kind of comfort, because at least it was a shelter, four walls and a roof for the wind to beat against.

"Oh, leave off that noise, do!" said Ellen. She was leaning back with her head against the wall, eyes closed. "Either play it proper, or leave it alone."

Kitchener gave the strings a final, defiant thwang and banged the instrument down on the floor beside him.

George gave Carrie one of his slow winks and for

once she felt able to smile back at him, because Ellen had her eyes closed.

"C'm'on, Carrie," Kitchener muttered, getting to his feet. She stood up.

"Where?"

"Up pier. See how Gamper's doing."

"You let him alone!" Ellen's voice was sharp, her eyes wide open now. "You let him get on with it. There's nothing you can do."

"Might be, Ellen," said George mildly. "You never know. They can always come away again if he don't want 'em."

Her head went back again.

"Don't take any notice of what *I* say," she said. "Do as you like. It'll probably make no difference one way or the other."

George gave Kitchener a nod, and next minute the two of them were outside with their faces to the wind, going up pier.

Chapter Ten

The sky over the sea was stormy. The shabby pier pavilion gleamed white against dark clouds edged with fans of light. As they walked up the pier it was as if they were walking into the heart of the storm.

"Or perhaps," Carrie thought, "it is because I'm going to meet the Last of the Magicians that it *seems* like it."

Their footsteps thudded on the wooden deck. Carrie was reminded of something.

"Did you find out whose those footsteps were?" she asked. "The ones in the dark?"

"Sam'el," replied Kitchener briefly.

"Oh, that's all right then," she said, relieved.

"Ma don't think so."

They had reached the last kiosk on the left now and were suddenly out of the shelter of the headland and plucked and ringed by eddying cross-currents of air, cold as water.

Kitchener pushed open the door and the Last Magician sat there wrapped in his mustard robes. Today he, too, was in storm, so wild in his looks that for a brief moment Carrie wondered if it were he who was spelling the clouds landwards and stirring whirlpools into the air.

"There's someone been at my spells!" he cried, without greeting.

"That's what you said yesterday, Gamper," said Kitchener. "They can't really be, you know."

"Watered down! Shrunk to nothing! Look at this!"

He seized a long-necked flask and waved it so that the pale green liquid it held leapt and fizzed against the glass walls.

"See?"

They both looked at it.

"See? Watered down so's it wouldn't fetch a daisy out of nowhere, let alone a tree! Look!"

He pulled out the stopper and dashed the liquid on to the floor before him. Hastily Carrie stepped back. She stared at the darkening splashes on the boards and hardly heard the words that the Great Pontifex was chanting like poetry. She looked up as he finished and saw that his arms were stretched out in front of him, hands outspread, palms down, fingers working and curling as if to force and pull a reluctant magic to spring up to his fingertips.

Kitchener nudged her and pointed down. Carrie looked back to the splashed floor and saw, impossibly, live green sprouting rootless from the boards, waving plants, green-branched, growing visibly inch by inch, stretching up towards the magician's beckoning fingers.

Abruptly he dropped his hands. All three of them stared at the magic he had done, though Carrie alone was awed by it. Kitchener had seen it all before, and the Great Pontifex himself was wild now with grief and fury.

"Oaks! Oaks, they are! *What's gone wrong?*"

"Pretty thin for oaks," admitted Kitchener. "*Could* the sea water've got into the spells, d'ye think?"

The magician seemed not to hear him. He began to stride furiously within the narrow confines of the kiosk. He paced like a caged lion, his mustard robes swirling so that he seemed to fill the whole space.

"It's my own fault!" he groaned. "My own fault! All those years of slip-shod summer shows, and never a thought for real magic, never so much as a new spell! So now my magic plays traitor to me. All my old spells gone now, for ever, slipped through my fingers!"

He wrung his hands in helpless anguish. In the silence the wind rattled the windows and moaned about the walls. The kiosk was darkening as the black clouds rolled above it. Carrie glanced at Kitchener and saw his face suddenly pinched and bleak. Her own mind reeled as she grasped the terror of it, and for a moment knew how it felt to be caught helpless, away from home and everything loved and familiar. And beyond that, even, was the certain knowledge that sinister forces were at work here at the pier's end, and only an old and tired magician to combat them. The Pontifexes were at sea in earnest now.

With an abrupt gesture the Great Pontifex flung out his arms with what sounded like a command and next moment the feeble shoots of the oaks had gone. He stamped a foot on the boards where they had been.

"They shot *down* easy enough, Gamper," offered Kitchener. "That part hasn't gone wrong."

"I do not understand," said the magician slowly. "And that, too, is a thing that has never happened to me before. I do not understand."

"It frightens me," he added, after a pause. "And even that is something new. After all, when one is the Last of the Magicians, one comes to think of oneself as more or less the Last Word, so to speak. And now it seems that there is something else—something that even *I* do not know. So the question must be asked—*who* knows?"

"*You* are the Last of the Magicians," Carrie said. "Who else *could* know?"

"Perhaps," he said slowly, leaving a pause that was filled by a distant mutter of thunder, "perhaps I am not the last, after all."

"But you are, Gamper, you are!" Kitchener cried. "There's only the Pontifexes been magicians for centuries, you told me so yourself!"

"Who else?" the old man muttered. "Who else?"

In the silence that followed footsteps could be heard approaching, and in the instant that Kitchener sprang and pushed the door shut, Carrie knew the answer.

"Uncle Sam'el!" she cried.

They stood and stared one at the other while the footsteps passed by the door.

"He comes down the pier nights," Kitchener said then, his voice hoarse. "It's him, right enough. Pa saw him clear last night—there's a moon rising. Every night since we've been here he's been down."

"Sam'el?" repeated the Great Pontifex. "*Sam'el?*"

"*All* the Pontifexes got some magic in 'em more or less—or used to," Kitchener said. "Pa says it's a dying strain—but how's he to know that Sam'el hasn't his veins *full* of it? More than"—he hesitated—"more than you, even, Gamper."

"Sam'el," said the Last of the Magicians again softly, slowly, weighing the word and its meaning together. There was a white flare of lightning. Kitchener and the old man, side by side, stared into it, great-eyed. Then the kiosk was suddenly darker than ever and the thunder crashed, thunder and echo running together in a prolonged muttering that sounded like a threat. The rain began to slant in from the sea so that the little kiosk was surrounded by voices and whispers, above, below, about, thunder, waves, wind, rain. Again the lightning flashed and Carrie found herself thinking, "Will this storm *ever* end?" because it all seemed to mean something—or the end of something.

"Day was when I could call a storm," said the Last of the Magicians, speaking to himself. "Call it up and make it dance for me."

"What do you mean, Gamper?" cried Kitchener. The old man looked at him.

"It's more than a party trick," he went on. "It's a great and terrible thing, to make a storm dance. It's not a thing to tinker with, no, on my soul it isn't. And you need reasons."

They could only guess what he was thinking of, but knew that he was groping, reaching out for an answer, and that the storm was part of it all, meant something. The little room was lit again and as swiftly dark.

"Is *this* storm yours, Gamper?" cried Kitchener. "Is it? Did *you* call it up?"

Carrie held her breath. Surely—surely not? The old man was shaking his head.

"I don't know, I don't know. . . ."

"Make it dance, Gamper!" cried Kitchener again, above the drumming of the wind and waves. "You must—it's our only chance! Try, Gamper, try!"

The magician straightened and drew his robes about him.

"Too late. You have to play a storm as you would a fish, draw it in, play your line. And it's too late now for that—the fish is swimming free. But there's something . . . something . . ."

"What? What?"

"There's the answer to a question in it, if the magic's strong enough. What was it, what was it . . . ? O how these spells dance in my old head. . . ."

Kitchener began, "I suppose—" but the magician put up a warning finger and Kitchener's mouth closed. Together he and Carrie stood pressed against the wall, watching the struggle.

Suddenly the Magician strode to the door and flung it wide. In came the storm, the wet, noisy wind and the smell of waves. He lifted his arms and stood spread against the streaked sky. Then his fingers began to work as they had done earlier.

Carrie and Kitchener crept up and looked out past him. At first there was nothing. The long fingers pulled and stretched, pulled and stretched. . . . The storm went its own way. It all seemed to go on and on

and on until again Carrie thought, "Will it ever end? Ever?"

Kitchener nudged her.

"Look! There!"

She followed his pointing finger and saw a cloud, one particular cloud. It was making itself under her very

eyes, drawing itself into a dreadful blackness and thick-ness. It was as if an ink blot had spread on blotting paper and was now shrinking back into itself again.

The cloud *was* like an ink spot now, perfectly round and black, and Carrie knew quite certainly that there had never before been a cloud like this. There is no geometry in the sky.

Now the cloud began to move, advancing towards the pier's end. It did not drift as clouds do, but rolled, like a ball. Carrie shut her eyes. She saw the lightning even through her eyelids, and almost in the same instant the thunder cracked, right overhead. She felt Kitchener's nudge and opened her eyes again.

The Great Pontifex had stepped right out into the storm. His yellow robes leapt about him as if they were alive. Carrie and Kitchener, standing in the doorway with the rain flying in their eyes, saw the clouds go by. It rolled in a straight line, with that same awful geometry, following a secret path over their heads, along the length of the pier, towards land.

"Where . . . ? Where . . . ?" wondered Carrie, swallowing the icy wind.

"Now!" cried the Great Pontifex, lifting his arms again, a great, ragged bird, poised for flight.

The cloud stopped. It hovered motionless as if a black ball had been thrown up and caught there, unable to fall. It stood right above the far end of the pier, the land end. It stood directly over the wet slated roof of the little toll house. There was a deafening clap of thunder right overhead.

"Uncle Sam'el!" came Kitchener's hoarse whisper by Carrie's ear. "Uncle Sam'el!"

Chapter Eleven

"It's like a tug of war," Carrie thought, "with them in the middle."

She stared down from her bedroom window at the pier, thinking of the Great Pontifex at one end and Sam'el at the other, matching spell for spell. Dusk was thickening at the sea's rim and with a shiver she wondered whether Sam'el's magic would gather strength with the darkness, and whether his footsteps would pass the little kiosk again that night while the Pontifexes listened, staring into the moonlight.

A cat yowled beneath the window and hastily Carrie banged it shut and dived for her bed, pulling the blankets over her ears. She lay remembering the spells she had watched the Last Magician working, after the storm. He had strewn angelica, caraway, rue.

"To keep off evil powers," Kitchener had whispered. "And catch old Sam'el if he comes creeping up pier again."

"No betany," the old man had muttered, sorting his bottles. "Betany none. O how I blame myself—don't I deserve it all? I have played traitor to my own magic—and now it plays traitor back to me."

It was then that he had lifted his head and looked straight into Carrie's eyes.

"*You* must help," he said.

"Me? But how? I—"

"Come tomorrow. There is a spell I must make. You'll come?"

His gaze was so deep and fierce that she could not answer, merely nodded dumbly. It was as if—and that was impossible—as if he were partly blaming *her*, as if it were *her* fault.

"And how could it be?" she thought now. "I'd never even set eyes on them before—except for their pictures, of course."

A little traitor voice in her head, just before she fell asleep, whispered:

"Ah, but you were *glad* they had come. And you wanted them to stay. *Still* want them to stay. . . ."

"No! No!" Carrie cried, and sat bolt upright in bed. The chintz curtains were lit orange. It was morning.

It was nearly eleven before she was able to escape. She hurried down towards the sea in the sharp October sunlight, with the bay glittering below and the auburn hills ringing it round. As she passed the iron railings of the school yard the children came running out to play, clattering into the quiet morning.

"Hey! You!" they shouted to her, and a group of them crowded up to the railings, grinning and staring. Suddenly Carrie wished she were one of them, and would even have given up pier, Pontifexes and all for the chance to run in amongst them and be one of them, instead of a stranger in a strange place. But she was cut off from them by the railings and her own shyness, and began to run towards her own world, the one she was familiar with and where she felt as if she belonged.

When she reached the pier entrance she waited for Sam'el Pontifex to appear with heart thudding. She had not seen him since the day before, since that terrible cloud had hung accusingly over the gate-house. She was relieved when at last he did come muttering forward to see that at least he *looked* the same, no more—and no less—a magician than he had ever seemed.

"Good morning," she said.

He did not return the greeting.

"No good you coming down here tomorrow," he told her, fumbling with his keys. "Nor the day after, for that matter, Pier closed."

"Closed?" What was he saying? "*Closed?*" she cried again.

He nodded, and she thought she caught a swift glee go over his face.

"But why?"

"Painters and decorators. Got to be done sometime. Ten year, since this last had a lick of paint, and the salt gets into it, bound to. Closed two week for painting and repairs. Look a treat when it's done, though."

He jerked his head as he spoke, and turning, Carrie saw a black board propped by the main turnstile. On it, written in chalk, was "Pier closed October 12th-26th for painting and repairs."

Desperately she searched for a loophole.

"But I've got a season ticket! I've paid for it—I can go on the pier whenever I want!"

He was shaking his head again.

"Makes no difference. Closed to *all*, public, season ticket or no season ticket. *Season* ticket don't mean anything, you know. You read the small print. 'Company reserves the right to refuse admission . . .' all that. Means

I can stop *anyone* going up pier, if I want. Authorized, I am."

Was it a threat? She could not see his face now, he had turned away and was going back into his house, as if he had already washed his hands of her.

She sped up the pier and as if her excitement were contagious the gulls gathered and screamed above her seven. Or perhaps by now they knew what to expect, even before she had worked the magical seven times and were ready to protest at the very sight of her.

She stood, breathless and invisible, looking about her. There was not a sign of the Pontifexes—nothing to see but her own shadow. Fleetingly she thought, "How very strange—I'm invisible, but I've got a shadow. My shadow's there, but I'm not. Queer!"

She went to the kiosk and knocked gently.

"It's me! Carrie!"

There was no reply. She knocked again—stranger still, the noise made by an invisible hand. She looked uneasily back over her shoulder. Only the gulls hung and scolded, lit beautifully white by the clear sun. Gently Carrie turned the knob and pushed. The door was locked!

She stood stunned by disappointment and fear. Gone? Or imprisoned? Had the Great Pontifex cast out his net among his swimming spells and caught at last the one that would set them free? Had they lain and wished and wished all through the long night till at last their wishing had worked its own magic and lifted them half a century back in time? Or was the silence a sinister one, mysteriously linked with the closing of the pier, perhaps? She stood irresolute. Should she go up the pier, or down?

Suddenly, with a strong, inner sense, she knew that the Pontifexes had *not* gone—not yet. And just as surely, she knew where they were. She started to run again up pier, shaking off the pursuit of the hoodwinked gulls, meeting the sun head on.

When she reached the last kiosk on the left she banged unceremoniously on the door.

"It's me! Carrie!"

The door opened and Kitchener stood there. Over his shoulder she met the stares of Ellen and George and could see the Last of the Magicians bending over a saucepan on the stove that Carrie herself had bought for Ellen.

"Thought you'd find us here," Kitchener said. "Inside, quick."

The door was closed again behind her, and she stood with the others, watching the Great Pontifex busy over his saucepans.

"What's he cooking?" she whispered.

"Spells," Kitchener whispered back. "Cooking spells. He's on to something."

The Last of the Magicians removed the pan from the heat and set it on the floor where it simmered and steamed as if by a power of its own. Carrie breathed in the sour, damp odour, and wondered fleetingly if you could be magicked by the mere *sniff* of a spell. She pressed the soles of her feet hard to the floor, resisting.

"Done, Gamper?" enquired George.

"Done."

"It don't *smell* very nice," observed Ellen. "But then it ain't for eating. Is it?" There was a faint note of alarm in the question.

"I wouldn't care if I had to swallow the lot," said Kitchener. "Not if it'd get us back again."

"You'll have to go tonight," said Carrie.

They all looked at her.

"Haven't you seen Sam'el? Didn't he tell you?"

"See *him*?" cried Ellen. "After what happened yesterday? Him? I don't ever want to set eyes on him again as long as I live. Didn't I tell you? Him with his—"

"Hush, Ellen," said George. "Let the girl speak. Tell us what?"

"About the pier. About its being closed. No one's to be allowed on after today, not for a whole fortnight. There's a notice up, saying it's closed for decorating and repairs. So I shan't be able to come—and what about you? They'll be painting the kiosks—they'll find out, they're bound to! You'll have to come off the pier, or you'll be trapped!"

There was a little silence. Then Ellen spoke.

"Never," she said. "Never."

"It's one thing or the other, Ellen," said George. "We've got to jump one way or the other. Tonight."

"If we come off pier, we're done," said Ellen flatly. "I know it. Done."

"Then it'll have to be the other," said George, and looked uncertainly at the Last Magician, who was bent unhearingly over his spells. "Come on, old girl, don't give in. The old man's *fizzing* with spells. He'll do it, you'll see."

Tears ran silently down Ellen's face. Kitchener stared desperately at the steaming spell.

"I might as well not be here," Carrie found herself thinking. "All they care about is getting back home."

And all of a sudden she found herself hoping, for the first time, that they *would* get back home, because she saw quite clearly that even if they stayed there was no hope that she would ever mean anything to them.

"I'll miss them," she thought, "but they won't miss me"—or only as prisoners miss a kindly jailer.

At that moment the Last of the Magicians looked up and their eyes met and Carrie had the extraordinary feeling that he knew exactly, *exactly* what she was thinking. And even more oddly, the knowledge was not uncomfortable at all, as one might have supposed, but a relief, almost comforting.

He turned his gaze to George.

"You go now," he said. "I want to speak to the girl."

George nodded and guided Ellen to the door. Kitchener raised his eyebrows at Carrie and followed. The door closed. Carrie, her heart thudding, heard their voices outside and then their footsteps receding down the pier. She could hear the windy air breaking round the tiny kiosk and far away, as if heard in a conch shell, the subdued, faint thunder of the waves. When she found courage to look back at the Last Magician, his eyes were on her.

"You will help?"

Carrie nodded.

"Never to see us again, that is what it will mean," he said. "Never. You will give us up, and we will go, never to return. You understand?"

Again she nodded.

"You are a kind of magician yourself," he said surprisingly then.

"Me?" she cried. "A *magician?*"

"There is more than one kind of magic," he said. "Flowers out of thin air, vanishing doves, snow in June —that is only a part of it. Sam'el found that out, too.

But is *your* magic stronger than his? He is an old man, and he clings tight—to everything, and to memories most of all."

"You mean—" Carrie's mind was reeling—"you mean *you*—all of you—are Sam'el's memories?"

"Does it seem impossible?"

"No-o. No," she replied slowly. "Not impossible. Is anything? Impossible, I mean?"

"That depends," he said. "One day you, too, will be old. Will you look back then, I wonder, and think that all *this* was impossible—that it didn't happen at all—that you dreamed it long ago, one far-off autumn by the sea when you were still a child, and believed in such things. Will you, I wonder?"

"Never!" cried Carrie. "Never! You *were* real—*are* real, I mean!"

"Oh, yes," he nodded. "We were—are."

"I'm all mixed up," she cried. "*You* must know. Are you real? Are you?"

He would say nothing, but merely looked at her, presenting her with her own question until in the end it was she who was forced to answer it.

"You are, you are!" she cried, and stamped her foot as if to force what she said to be the truth.

"Good." He nodded approvingly. "Now there is very little left to be done. The spell is ready," he nodded his head towards the steaming green liquid, "and come to-night we shall all be home—there for the wishing."

"*My* wishing?" asked Carrie. But she already knew the answer.

Chapter Twelve

Carrie walked very slowly back down the pier, giving herself a chance to gather her thoughts. The Last of the Magicians had told her the part she had to play in tonight's escape, and she had promised willingly.

"I *do* wish you home, oh I do, I *do*," she had said.

"We shall go at midnight. Sam'el will be sleeping, perhaps, but even in his dreams he will not let go. Your wishing must be stronger than his—the spell alone is powerless. Do you understand?"

She had nodded, already pitting herself against the old man at the pier's end who would hold the Pontifexes captive for ever, greedy as he was for their company.

"It will not be easy," the Magician had warned her then. "Sam'el is a kind of magician too, remember, and it was partly his wishing that has brought us here. There will be a battle."

Carrie fleetingly pictured the pier at midnight and the desperate tug of war in the moonlight over the waves, and shuddered.

"But how can I come?" she had cried. "The house

will be locked and the streets will be dark—and I'll be afraid, I know I will!"

The Last of the Magicians had stretched out a long, lean palm, and Carrie saw, lying in it, a round yellow pill, sugar-coated like a sweet.

"Take this. When you go to bed, eat it. That is all you have to do."

She had stared at him and taken the tablet, pushing it deep into her pocket. And now, walking slowly back down pier, she felt for it with her fingers, and thought of all the questions she wished she had asked him.

"But perhaps it is better not to know the answers," she thought. "Perhaps there *aren't* even any answers, with real magic. If the magic works, then that is enough."

She hastened her steps towards the first kiosk where she could see the door standing open and empty boxes piled up outside. Kitchener was leaning against the door of the photograph kiosk opposite, keeping look-out, she supposed.

She called his name, and he turned, took his hands from his pockets and came towards her.

"What did the old man say?" he demanded, before he had even reached her. She shook her head.

"A lot of things. He wants me to help."

Kitchener nodded.

"It's to do with wishing, isn't it?" He regarded her curiously. "Was it *you* that brought us here?"

She began to deny it, but he brushed her protests aside.

"Oh, it's all right. I shan't get mad at you. *You* weren't

to know. Any case, it could only've been *partly* you. It's him"—with a jerk of his head down pier—"that really started it. Old devil!"

"Kitchener!"

"He *is*. Ma was right about him. Took us prisoner and meant to keep us up pier for ever—it's clear as day. And we ain't home yet. How do *we* know what he's got up his sleeve?"

"I feel sorry for him," Carried said.

"*Sorry?*"

"Being so lonely. He didn't mean any harm."

"Trying to keep people against their wills? *That's* harm, ain't it? Kidnapping, it's called. You can go to prison for it—and serve him right if he did. And don't you start sticking up for him. It's you that's got to fight him."

Again the picture of the moonwashed pier rose in her mind and hastily Carrie pushed it away.

"What are they doing?" she asked, changing the subject. They were level with the kiosk now and inside she could see George and Ellen, both on their hands and knees.

"Packing. Getting ready."

Carrie peered in and saw with a pang that the walls were bare, the boxes undraped, the bedding in piles. The Pontifexes were packing in earnest and Carrie knew for certain now that it was all over.

George raised a hot red face and Ellen sat back on her heels, brushing the flyaway hair from her eyes.

"If there's one thing worse than unpacking," she said, "it's packing."

But her eyes were bright, she was brimming with excitement. Carrie remembered the canvas bag of money and opened the duffle bag she was carrying.

"Here," she said, holding out the bag. "Better take this. I shan't be coming again."

Ellen, her hand outstretched for the bag, dropped it suddenly.

"Not coming? You must! Mustn't she, George? Ponty says it's only your wishing can save us now—he *needs* you, for his spell to work!"

"What I meant is, that it's the last *real* time. How do we know what will happen tonight? Do *you* know?"

The three of them looked at her, and George shook his head.

"Oh, what a queer time it's all been," sighed Ellen then, absently getting to her feet and folding a shawl. "*How* long have we been here? Two days, two hours, two centuries? How will it *seem* to us when we get back? Shall we even remember?"

Carrie saw what she meant. Would the Pontifexes step back into their time and take up their lives as if nothing had ever happened? Or would Ellen perhaps say to George:

"O George, I had the queerest dream last night", and begin to tell it, until George interrupted her, saying excitedly, "Would you believe that, old girl—I had the very same dream myself!"

"You all keep going on as if we *was* going to get back," said Kitchener. "But how do we *know*?"

For a moment no one spoke. The question hovered about them.

"It'll be the end of the world for us if we don't," said Ellen at last. Carrie realized that they were looking at her, all three of them, expectantly, almost beseechingly.

"You will—oh, you will!" she cried, and hastily averted her own eyes and felt her heart begin to beat suffocatingly in her throat.

"Game's over, really, isn't it?" said George.

"Yes." Carrie looked at his serious face and wondered how much he knew, for all his winking and whistling and devil-may-care shrugs. "The game's over."

"It's not that we haven't enjoyed it." It was Ellen, standing very straight now and speaking politely, like a child thanking an adult for a party.

"O *ma!* What a *liar!*"

"You be quiet!" She whirled on him, yellow beads in flight. "You watch your manners! We ain't home yet, you know. Mind what you say!"

She turned to Carrie and again the face became polite, *anxiously* polite.

"It's been ever so nice, meeting you," she said. "Really it has."

"O dear," Carrie thought. "She wants to shake hands!"

She held out her own hand, and then George offered his. It was terrible.

"Now we are strangers again," Carrie thought, "back at the beginning again." She remembered the Pontifexes as they had been that first evening, and the way they had watched her, warily, alert to danger.

"Kitchener!" said Ellen warningly.

Obediently he, too, stuck out his hand. Carrie took it and that, too, was the end of that. George cleared his throat.

"Ships that pass in the night," he observed, awkwardly, as if feeling bound to say something to pass the moment off.

Carrie nodded. Suddenly the sight of them, standing by their half-packed luggage, familiar but already withdrawn, became unbearable.

"Goodbye!" she cried. "I do hope—oh, I *do* hope—oh, I don't know what I'd have done without you!"

She made for the door, and heard Ellen's voice.

"Here, take this. It's for you!"

Carrie turned back and saw that she was holding out the string of yellow beads, the beads that were almost part of Ellen herself—a kind of extension.

"Take them!" said Ellen again. Carrie took them.

"Thank you. Thank you—oh, goodbye!"

This time she did go, and heard Kitchener's voice floating after her:

"'Bye, Carrie! Good luck!"

She ran, ran faster away from them than she had ever run towards them, and crossed the line of the seven times seven and heard the gulls go into clamour. As she ran the gulls' cries and the salt taste of her tears mingled so that they seemed one and the same thing.

Gasping for breath and wiping a sleeve across her blinded eyes she looked up and saw that she had nearly reached the end of the pier. Her glance took in the tall figure of a man standing just beyond the turnstiles. He swam into a blur, but she brushed her arm across her eyes and looked again, caught by something about the turn of the head and the hands buried deep in the pockets.

"It is! It is!" she cried, and next minute was back on land and caught in his arms, strange and familiar at once, a memory made real. The arms tightened about her.

"Here, Carrie. Hey, sweetheart, what is it? Didn't they tell you I was coming?"

"Yes, but—yes, but I thought you'd gone! I thought you'd gone for ever! And I want to go home!" she sobbed. "I want to go home!"

He had lifted her now, right up so that she was level with his face and she could clasp her arms tightly about his neck and feel him safe and unbelievably *there* again, the whole world miraculously in order once more.

Gradually her sobs quietened and slowly he lowered her to the ground. Then he took her hand and they turned towards the road up to the town.

"Come on," he said. "We're *going* home. Really home. All of us."

Chapter Thirteen

Carrie went to bed late that night. She had sat in the basement kitchen—transformed now into a place both friendly and familiar—and listened while the others talked. Now and again her thoughts had wandered momentarily to the Pontifexes and the night ahead. But the present reality was so strong and warm that they had only hovered about the edges of her thoughts, shadows of themselves.

Her father brought out photographs of the house they were to live in. She had sat with them on the table before her until they were photographed on her own mind and she could already think of the four-square house with its sharply sloping roof as home.

Now, as she sat on the edge of her bed and stared at the Magician's pill, it was still an effort to think of the Pontifexes at all—it was as if they had already gone home. But they had not. They were now a single step away from home, a dangerous single step over time and waves.

She went to the window and drew back the curtain. With a shock she met the full stare of the moon. It hung out there in the misty half light of its own making, more full, more *meaning*ful than any moon she had ever seen before. She met the stare for a long time before moving her gaze down to the lights of the town, pale tonight, bleached and somehow pointless, like a lighted bulb in a sunny room.

Tonight she could see the pier itself, poised in its enigmatic stride from land to sea, from sea to land. The roofs of the kiosks were a dulled, far-off silver. At the far end the pavilion appeared softly edged and insubstantial as if it had been cut adrift and were swimming free. Looking at last reluctantly towards the land end, Carrie saw the gatehouse and the light burning in an upper room.

"He's still awake," she thought, and shivered. But even the terror was oddly blurred now, not so much *real* terror as a necessary terror that she must act out if she were to play her part.

She dropped the curtain, went back to the bedside, stared at the round yellow tablet for a moment, then put it quickly in her mouth. As the sugary outer coat dissolved, she tasted chocolate. She got into bed, turned on her side, and reached for the switch of the bedside light. As she did so, her eyes fell on the string of yellow beads.

"Ellen's," she thought. "Mine now."

Then the light was out and it was as if she had cast anchor and was adrift now in the darkness.

She was adrift in the darkness. She was standing by the entrance to the pier itself and as she stood slowly the darkness thinned and the scene was washed in moonlight. Before her were the shining metal arms of the turnstiles, locked, fixed, impassable. In an upper window of the gatehouse the light still shone. Sam'el Pontifex was keeping the long night watches, keeping guard over his prisoners.

"How shall I pass?" Carrie asked herself. Impossible to knock at the door. "I must climb," she thought.

She looked about her instinctively to see if she were watched. It was then that she noticed that she had no shadow. Why she should have noticed she could never afterwards tell—perhaps nothing ever *is* noticed until it is missed. Slowly she wheeled in the full light of the moon. *She had no shadow*.

"And I always had before," she told herself, "even when I was invisible. I'm still me, but I have no shadow." She stretched out her arms, savouring the sensation.

Suddenly the light brightened and looking up she saw that another light had appeared, in a downstairs window of the gatehouse. She waited. She stood for one minute, two, three . . .

The door opened and Sam'el Pontifex came out. Quietly he shut the door behind him.

Carrie heard the rattle of keys and the creak of the pier gate. He passed through and left it swinging open behind him. Slowly he set off up pier, an old man with keys, a jailer.

Carrie waited another minute and passing noiselessly through the open gate followed at the same pace. She kept her eyes on his back, keeping her distance. Then without warning Sam'el halted in his tracks. He stopped abruptly as if frozen by some sight or sound ahead.

Carrie, hastening her own pace, drew close behind

and still he stood there, rigid, motionless. She noticed then that Sam'el, too, had no shadow. She saw that the place where he stood was the dividing line between the tarmac and the wooden floor of the deck, between land and sea.

Stopping close behind him she looked ahead and saw for the first time the Pontifexes. They stood perfectly still as if in tableau by the open door of their kiosk. They stood shadowless. The Last of the Magicians, his mustard robes bleached in the moonlight, stared over to where Sam'el stood, and his eyes flashed silver.

"You can come no further!" he cried. "I have made a spell, a certain spell, and you can stir neither hand nor foot!"

The waves muttered and sucked far away down below. Carrie held her breath.

"*You* move!" Sam'el's voice was high and triumphant. "You move, if you can!"

Motionless the Pontifexes stood and to Carrie, standing at a distance, their pale faces were blanks and she could only guess at their despair.

The Last Magician had his head tilted back as if he were watching something in the sky. Carrie looked up, right above the pier-keeper's head, and saw them.

The gulls were gathering. They came stealthily, as if with muffled wings. Their pallid shapes rose from the shadowy clefts of the Great Strindel or swam out of the misty light above the estuary. They *blossomed*, out of nowhere, it seemed, and came silently together till at last they were hanging right above the pier itself in a marvellous, hushed cloud.

"Does he *see* them?" wondered Carrie.

"*I've* got spells!" cried Sam'el then. "Spell for spell I'll match you! Here we'll stand for ever, then! *For ever*, do you hear?"

"Let go, Sam'el," came the voice of the Last Magician.

"Never!" cried the gatekeeper. "Never! I've got you fast, and I'll keep you! You're mine! Mine!"

They stood locked, all five of them, as if frozen under a thin silver rime. The cloud of gulls seethed as silent wings rode on air. Only the world went on, the clouds trailing over the moon, the water tossing and splashing underfoot, and then Carrie, too, miraculously found herself moving. She walked out free on to the wooden deck and stood between them and heard herself say, without the least idea why she was saying it:

"No. You're mine. All of you. And *I* set you free!"

In one crowded instant she saw the incredulous, joyful faces of the Pontifexes, heard Sam'el's scream of fury and saw black shadows spring out from their feet, all of them.

And as they were set free and made visible, and in the very moment when Sam'el started to move towards the Last Magician, arm raised in threat, the gulls were thrown into their old clamour.

They broke out of the sky in a great storm of screams and feathers. Carrie heard Sam'el's cry and saw him put up his arms as if to shield himself. She stepped aside and had a last glimpse of the Pontifexes as if behind a curtain of whirling snow, and was then herself adrift in darkness again, the crying of the gulls still in her ears.

When she woke, she could still hear the gulls. She lay listening to them, as she had done that first morning. Her eyes travelled over the now familiar room, and came to rest at last on her own luggage, still only half-unpacked. Inside her head she seemed to hear the voice of the Last of the Magicians:

"You are a kind of Magician yourself," he was saying.

She lay there smiling.

"I think perhaps I am," she thought. And then, "I can start packing now. . . ."